Leonard Brown

Poems of the Prairies

Leonard Brown

Poems of the Prairies

ISBN/EAN: 9783337408138

Printed in Europe, USA, Canada, Australia, Japan

Cover: Foto ©Andreas Hilbeck / pixelio.de

More available books at **www.hansebooks.com**

POEMS OF THE PRAIRIES.

LEONARD BROWN.

We care not whether the verse be rugged or not, so long as it is *American*.
* * * * Only let it be the care of the present to lay the foundation of a national
poetry, which will then insure a national literature.

W. CLARK RUSSELL.

NEW EDITION.

DES MOINES:

PUBLISHED BY REDHEAD AND WELLSLAGER,

41 COURT AVENUE.

1868.

RIVERSIDE, CAMBRIDGE:

STEREOTYPED AND PRINTED BY

H. O. HOUGHTON AND COMPANY.

To

M. ARATHUSA ALLEN,

AS A

TOKEN OF RESPECT AND GRATITUDE.

PREFACE TO THE SECOND EDITION.

——◆——

THIS book has been kindly noticed by the press and favorably received by the people. Good verses may be written here as well as elsewhere. " Labor omnia vincit" is the author's motto —

> " Incessant pains
> The end obtains."

Certainly it is just on the part of " critics " to require that the " POEMS OF THE PRAIRIES " be perfect, — not containing a faulty line, word, or syllable. It would seem strange if here, on the frontier, a volume of verses should not be written more perfect in all things than the most finished productions of Tennyson, the poet of ease and leisure. One who toils for his daily bread, when he snatches a moment from labor in which to write, is expected to surpass, in the beauty of his diction, the most polished of the poets of ancient or modern days, or he must be lashed by a set of fools! Pope says : —

> " Let such teach others who themselves excel,
> And censure freely who have written well."

And —

> " Whoever thinks a faultless piece to see,
> Thinks what ne'er was, nor is, nor e'er shall be ;

> In every work regard the writer's end,
> Since none can compass more than they intend;
> And if the means be just, the conduct true,
> Applause, in spite of trivial faults, is due."

And Dryden —

" True judgment in poetry, like that in painting, takes a view of the whole together, whether it be good or not; and where the beauties are more than the faults, concludes for the poet against the little judge."

The author hopes that his book merits fully the praise bestowed upon it by the leading journals of the West. But above all words of commendation he esteems the friendship of that benevolent and public spirited man of wealth, B. F. Allen, through whose liberality this book was first published. Indeed, no enterprise is undertaken for the public good in Iowa but he is a worker in it and contributes largely to it. He seems to be impressed that there is in these poems something of excellence. May his kindly efforts in behalf of literature, in the beautiful State lying between the great rivers, be, at least, partially rewarded through the humble instrumentality of the author of this book, whose reliance is not on himself, nor on man, but on God, who, in His providence, sometimes chooses the lowly of this world as His means of accomplishing His high purposes. The continued friendship of this good man, and the favor of God, may enable the author of this little work to accomplish that of which his countrymen will one day be proud; for he has it in mind to undertake a work of great magnitude and labor, which, if successful, will be of national utility.

The greater part of the poems in this volume were written before the war, and while the author was quite young. He wrote "*Our Country*" when he was nineteen years old. The learning he has acquired was sought under many difficulties and discouragements. A blacksmith's apprentice in his youth, he had few advantages of early instruction from books; but he wishes what he has written to stand upon its merits alone, and he does not purpose using the unpromising circumstances of life under which he grew up as a means of magnifying his poetry. If it is good, it will, in time, be fully appreciated; and if not good, the author will meet resignedly his then deserved doom — oblivion. But he is most sanguine in his anticipations of success. He believes that all who read this book carefully and impartially, will find in it something to commend, and that it will do good in giving hope and encouragement to the young in pursuit of knowledge and virtue. He believes that the highest aim of the poet should be to teach virtue and love of country, God, and man; and that writers of the school of Byron are not destined to live always in the affections of men, but that virtue is immortal as God and the soul of man; that our country is destined to embrace the continent, and patriotism will not die. The writer believes that his poems are not entirely devoid of that polish so characteristic of classic English poetry, especially of that of Pope; but he is well aware that he has not attained to that degree of perfection in the art which he hopes time and practice may yet give him. He is self-taught; only he believes that God has breathed into his heart the songs that are struggling for utterance. He has all along kept his eye on the ancient poets. Hesiod, the most ancient, wrote of " *Works and Days.*" The common scenes of life, and the real interests of men, and not clouds, fairies, and *moon-shine*, were of old the themes of poets. Poetry is mighty. The Scriptures are mainly poetry, and the world is taught by poets. An orator of the olden time says : —

" Therefore, rightly does our own great Ennuis call poets holy; because they seem to be recommended to us by some special gift and liberality of the gods. Let then, judges, this name of poet, this name which no barbarians, even, have ever disregarded, be holy in your eyes, — men of cultivated minds as you all are. Rocks and deserts reply to the poet's voice. Savage beasts are often moved and arrested by song."

THE AUTHOR.

Des Moines, *September 25th,* 1867.

CONTENTS.

PATRIOTIC POEMS.

SATIRICAL POEMS.

POESY. A LYRIC.

MISCELLANEOUS POEMS.

EARLIER POEMS.

TO B. F. ALLEN.

Freedom triumphant! and the " Sovereign "
  Who bought and sold his human chattels " hurled
  With hideous ruin " to the nether world,
Our land is left replete with honest men —
With *rich* men *patriots* — noblemen indeed, —
  Loving Religion, Liberty, and Fame.
  Allen, with gratitude I speak thy name,
For I have had thy kindly help in need ;
Thou hast a loyal faith in God and man ;
  Jehovah's name thou honorest ; and to thee
  Is *first* of all God's works — *Humanity.*
" *My Heavenly Father, with thy aid I can*
Succeed ! " — God prompts kind acts, — the poet lives.
To Allen thanks, — all praise to God he gives.

TO M. A. A.

If in ourselves we have not faith, will men
Have faith in us? God early gave me hope.
Columbus at the court of Ferdinand
Still pressed his suit, till Isabella gave
The needed aid, — pledging her costly jewels.
The light of God shone on him, and revealed
Distinctly to his view the Hesp'rian world.

PATRIOTIC POEMS.

OUR COUNTRY.

O N a shore far remote, in days now long
    past,
    Some God-fearing men, whose possessions
      were vast,
Bade adieu to their homes and fields of bright
    grain,
In a small ship of burden to cross the rough main.
Nor treasures, nor plunder they sought o'er the
    seas;
The flag of Religion they spread to the breeze,
Displaying this motto, expressive and odd, —
" Rebellion to tyrants is duty to God."
Away from oppression and Britain they bore,
And landed on Holland's republican shore.

Beyond the broad ocean America lay,
Where the sun drives his chariot at close of the
    day;
Savage men and wild beasts had there their
    abode;
But there, too, the Temple of Liberty stood.

The heroes of faith saw its dome from afar,
And hailed it again as their beaconing star.
They rode on the bosom of Ocean once more;
They came to a bleak and a desolate shore;
No Dido received them at Old Plymouth Rock;
At the doors of no princely mansion they knock;
Old Boreas, winter-robed, stood on the strand,
To welcome the coming of that pilgrim band.
O Puritan fathers, your names we revere;
How great were your labors and sufferings here;
How sorely harassed by your wild Indian foes;
How Famine oppressed you with direful woes!
Your God you heard whisper in every breeze
That passed o'er the mountains or sang through
    the trees, —
" Ye children of Freedom, press on to the prize;
A glorious nation from you shall arise!"

The axe of the woodman advances its strokes;
The forest of ages is shorn of its oaks;
And thousands of freemen dwell on the bright
    shore,
Where the rod of Oppression may reach them no
    more.

Hermea, lovely maiden, given sweetly to rest,
Once dreamed that a serpent lay coiled on her
    breast;
No dreams of dread reptiles our fathers harassed,
But worse than a Hydra assailed them at last, —
A desperate tyrant, whose treacherous aim

Was the spirit of freedom to thoroughly tame.
Go tame the proud bison, the prairie that roams;
Tame him as he breathes the free air of your
    homes.

" Brother, please hand me my scabbard and knife;
I go to the conflict; I 'm bound for the strife!
Dearest maiden, cease weeping; good mother, fare-
    well;
Those proud British foemen I, too, must help
    quell;
I know my loved sisters may suffer for bread;
I know, too, my father all gory lies dead!
Did not he with brave Warren, the last on the
    field,
His life for his children most willingly yield?
Shall I, proudly boasting his blood in my veins,
Shrink back while a hope for my country re-
    mains?
Away to our chieftain, my steed must be fleet!
The chieftain so gallant at Braddock's defeat!
Bold hearts now assemble; their swords glitter
    bright;
They go where he leads in defense of the right,
'Neath the banner of freedom — the eagle on
    high —
To conquer, and triumph, or willingly die!"

" Go, son, saith the matron, go join in the strife;
She sends you who loves you, who gave you
    your life; —

2

'Gainst famine we cheerfully trust in His care
Who looks to the sparrow that falls through the air.
This Bible take with you wherever you roam,
That God may protect you and guide you safe
    home,
If not to our dwelling on earth here of love,
To a mansion more pleasing in Heaven above."

What tyrant e'er conquered a spirit like this?
What Gesler could humble brave Tell of the
    Swiss ?
No bravery or fortitude ever was shown,
By any bold people, surpassing our own ;
The dread British Lion they humbled in pride,
The monster Oppression fell gasping and died,
And reward for their labors thus fully they gained ;
The great " Declaration of Freedom " maintained !

They said, " We have triumphed ; this land is our
    own ;
But then must there here be established a throne ?
How soon would we rue that perfidious power !
How soon would be banished from Freedom's fair
    bower.
Contemplate the picture, instructive and true,
That pages historic exhibit to view !
Behold there all Monarchy shrouded in gloom,
And grim Aristocracy, black as the tomb !
At the top of the canvas old Greece stands
    alone, —
Oh gaze on her splendor that for ages has shone

The light of the world! the pride of mankind!
Most radiantly glorious! of all most refined!
There thought was unfettered; all the land a great
    school, —
Man rose to perfection — Why? — *The people
    bore rule!*
Look, too, at proud Rome, the Plebeian in power,
Subduing the world, as it were, in an hour!"

So led were our fathers a Republic to choose;
But the child of their choice did monarchs amuse!
For the day it should die and be cast in the sea,
They planned to themselves quite a grand jubilee.
Since then the "weak babe" has a Hercules
    grown;
At his look now dread Monarchy quakes on her
    throne;
A giant Antæus in his arms has been crushed;
The voice of oppressors to silence is hushed;
The world, we may say, he bears up with all
    ease;
Golden apples are snatched from the Hesper-
    ides, —
Golden apples of freedom, fairest fruit ever known,
Through him shall all nations receive as their
    own!

My Country, I love thee, thy prairies and hills;
Thy broad, flowing rivers and murmuring rills;
Thy greatness be sung to the true poet's lyre,
In strains that such freedom alone can inspire!

American youth, behold where you stand!
To you must be given the care of this land!
Prepare for your calling; be worthy the trust;
Let not our proud banner be dragged in the dust!
Then banish ambition, and avarice, and pride,
That a true *public spirit* may ever abide.
'T' was the loss of this anchor that sunk mighty
　　Rome.
Be ever, Columbia, the patriot's home!

June, 1857.

IOWA.

PART FIRST.

—◆—

THE PAST.

A MORNING'S MEDITATION ON THE BANKS OF THE DES MOINES.

"Every human heart is human."

LONGFELLOW.

It is a pleasant summer morn;
Gently waves the growing corn;
From the leafy groves, the air
Wafts a fragrance everywhere;
And along the eastern sky
Lovely sunbeams greet the eye,
That o'er fairy clouds diffuse
Tinges of unnumbered hues.
At length the Sun himself appears,
Great herald of revolving years!
And smiles as radiant and young
As when immortal Ossian sung!
Thou giver of the lovely day!
From thee I turn my face away;
I cannot for a moment brook
Thy searching glance, thy piercing look;
But gladly on this stream I gaze,

From which thy ever-splendent rays
Have driven the mists, that o'er it spread
Dark as the living cloud so dread
That hovered o'er a pleasant land
As one of old " stretched out his hand."
I love upon these banks to stray
Thus at the sweet approach of day,
And gazing on the beauteous stream
To wander in poetic dream.
I hear a distant lonely sound,
That carries sadness all around!
'T is of the ever mournful dove
Sighing for her absent love.
Here let me recline my head
Pensive on this mossy bed,
Nearer by the river side,
Where waters murmur as they glide, --
That my ear may catch again
The ever tender, saddening strain ;
For it moving, moaning on
Recalls to mind the loved ones gone,
Whom bright angels bore away
To realms of everlasting day.
Now there comes a deeper moan ;
'T is sadder than a dying groan !
The waves are sighing as they flow, —
Methinks are singing as they go,
A mournful, melancholy lay, —
The dirge of a departed day.

SONG OF THE WAVES.

The dead! The dead! The dead are here!
Ask not the day, ask not the year,
When loved ones bore them on the bier,
And laid them lowly in the ground,
And made the monumental mound!
Age hath followed ages fast;
The streams new channels formed and past,
And deep through rocks have worn their way
Since they mouldered into clay:

    The patriot brave, who thoughtful stood
    Looking down upon this flood;
    His country's wrongs were in his breast;
    Eye-flashing rage his look expressed,
    Revenge resolving on her foes —
    His blood redeemed her from her woes;
    Rest thee, O warrior, in repose!

The lovely maid who oft of yore
Gathered wild flowers on this shore,
Strolling in the happy grove,
Caroling a song of love;
Now bathing in the limpid waves;
Now in the cooling breeze she laves,
And gazing, like fair Eve, with pride
In the pellucid mirror-tide,
Viewing there her form and face,
All radiant with every grace,

She modestly and sweetly smiled, —
Behold her, Nature's lovely child!
She sleeps in death, low in the ground,
Beneath the ancient grassy mound.

And the Bard (whose song was given —
A light to guide from Earth to Heaven) —
There lies, with harp beneath his head,
Unstrung, decayed; its voice is dead!
To all resistless was its spell,
While sang the agéd Minstrel
The sylvan beauties of these streams;
The hero's wondrous deeds and dreams;
Love's longing looks, and soul-born smiles;
Her hidden hopes, and winsome wiles.
And shall its strains no more arise
Rejoicing to these western skies,
As wild birds sing, and waters flow,
And lovely prairies verdant grow?

O stream, how touching is thy lay!
And must great worth thus find decay,
And all man's glory fade away?

THE INDIAN.

From thee has gone the Indian brave;
Nor Sac, nor Fox beholds thy wave;
And yet upon thy margin green
Not long ago his lodge was seen,
In its wild, fantastic form, —

An humble covert from the storm ;
His trembling maize-field stood hard by ;
His bean and melon-patch was nigh ;
His pony fed upon the plain, —
See all the Indian had of gain !
And well content, when thus supplied ;
His every want was satisfied ;
His happy heart, with love of gold,
Had not begun to rot or mould ;
The needy stranger at the door
Was welcome to the red man's store.

I have often in delight
Seen the meteor at night,
With a glorious display,
Darting hurriedly away
Across the star-bespangled sky,
Joying in its course on high ;
It soon vanished from my view,
Buried in the boundless blue,
Leaving not a trace behind
Of the glory it resigned.

The Indian passed away, and lo !
What is left behind to show
That he drew Ulysses' bow ?
He often earned immortal fame ;
But what perpetuates his name ?
What monument remains to tell
Where, like Leonidas, he fell ?
Many an unknown field may be

A Marathon or Thermopylæ!
All he for ages said or did
Must ever lie in darkness hid;
Only here a grassy sod
Marks where once his wigwam stood,
And some little pits remain
That in Winter held his grain.
The sweet-flowing " Chicaqua," *
And the bright " Asipala," †
Lost are these names to rivers clear;
While the ruder ones we hear
Ungrateful to the poet's ear!
Still round the graves, and o'er the dead
Some mossy bark and boards are spread;
It was of these the mourners made
A little wigwam for his shade,
To be for it a sheltering home,
Until he o'er the prairie roam,
And, wandering, find the rolling flood,
That flows this side the happy wood —
The ever-joyful hunting ground
In which exhaustless game is found.
There — if his course of life had been
Bright and free from trace of sin —
He would cross the trembling log
With his ever-faithful dog,
And join his comrades in the chase,
And live in endless happiness.
If like the hound, he come there hoarse
From baying on a vicious course,

* Skunk River.   † Raccoon River.

He cannot reach the happy wood,
But quickly falls into the flood;
Then rolling, howling, in the tide.
He struggles for the nearest side, —
Every effort is in vain,
To reach the woodland or the plain;
The rushing wave, with mighty roar,
Sweeps him to a barren shore; —
Degraded there in poverty,
He finds eternal misery.

Meandering the prairies green
Still the Indian path is seen,
Bending over woody hills,
Crossing sweetly flowing rills.
Wandering near it thoughtfully,
Imaginings most pleasantly,
Like visions of the fairest kind,
Came on bright before my mind.

A CEREMONY.

I saw a long, lamenting train
Of women passing o'er the plain,
Appearing as they had before
Annually in days of yore;
Moaning matrons moving on,
And weeping widows, one by one;
Sorrowing sisters were the last
In the procession as it passed —
So very sad; and yet, I ween,

There never was a lovelier scene
Than they presented to my sight,
Performing this religious rite,
Of bearing gifts, and proffering
To their dead an offering.
All the maidens passed along
Chanting wild and mournful song.

THE INDIAN MAIDS' SONG.

"Again returns the day of sadness!
Again returns the day of gladness!
The Great Spirit has bereft us;
The Great Spirit has not left us!
Friends are gone; nor do we greet them;
Friends are gone; but we shall meet them;
Good Spirits hover o'er us lightly;
Good Spirits shine above us brightly;
From the rocks and caves they started;
From the rocks and caves departed,
When they heard us weeping, moaning, —
When they heard us sighing, groaning;
On their swan-like wings came fleeting;
On their swan-like wings came greeting —
Greeting us, and now are near us;
Greeting us with words to cheer us:
' Weep no more; be not fearful;
Weep no more; be calm and cheerful —
The Great Spirit loves you dearly;
The Great Spirit knows how nearly
His good children are unto him;
His good children all shall view him;
View him and dwell with him ever;

View him and be parted never;
Never more shall sigh in sorrow;
Never more shall dread the morrow!
Let this, then, be day of gladness;
Let it not be one of sadness;
Weep no more; be not fearful;
Weep no more; be calm and cheerful'!"

And appearing truly fair,
With their zephyr-combéd hair
Flowing over shoulders bare,
And the dark expressive eye,
Hopeful turned toward the sky, —
Angel form; romantic dress;
They were queens in loveliness!
Now all have reached the burial place,
And there I can more clearly trace
The deepening of their wild distress, —
The dead they mournfully address!
The Mother thus: —

      "My babe so dear!
My little darling, Oh, come near;
Let me again behold thy face,
And with fond kisses thee embrace!
Something I see most lovely, fair,
And bright, above me in the air, —
'T is sure, 't is sure my very child!
Come nearer still, thou vision mild,
And never, never more depart!
Oh, could I press thee to my heart!
Thanks, thanks to Onwenah above,
Who thus would spare thee in his love,

To calm thy mother's stormy breast,
To give her wearied spirit rest;
For now, no more, no more I weep!
My soul with rapture glories deep;
Since I behold on wings of light,
My child, so beautiful and bright!"

The widow: —

           "O, my husband, why,
Why wilt thou not descend from high,
And to my sorrowing soul convey
Of thy bright joy a single ray!
Forlorn, forlorn, I here must be!
O dearest, dearest, pity me,
And take me once again to thee!
Enwrap me in thy arms once more,
And on the bright, celestial shore,
Where nothing in immortal groves
May ever more distract our loves!
O husband! when with flagging pace
Thou art returning from the chase,
Oppressed with toil; thy arrows spent;
Thy back with fleshy burden bent;
Who now doth strain her anxious sight
To see thee gain the woody height,
And, when thy shadow there doth stray,
So soon is on her willing way
To bear a part of thy dull load
And lead thee to the fair abode,
Where viands for thee she hath blest,
That thou may'st eat and sweetly rest?
And when thou liest wrapped in sleep
Doth o'er thee midnight vigil keep,

And, as the moon, serenely bright,
Enchants the wigwam with her light —
Reveals the features of thy face,
Who doth thee lovingly embrace?"

" Brothers, [thus the sisters said,]
Return from wandering with the dead!
Receive this offered gift of ours;
Receive these lovely prairie flowers!
We lay them gently on the tomb
To please you with their sweet perfume;
They are the fairest we can find
Disporting in the prairie wind!
On plucking them they seemed to say,
' We gladly go with you away
To form the happiest bouquet!
A token, beautiful, of love
From friends below to friends above.'
And other presents, too, we bring
With this our kindly offering —
Your bows and arrows here we place;
For you may need them in the chase;
And your ornaments so fair,
We now leave them in your care.
On your graves no wilding grows;
Pebbles mark where you repose;
Pebbles that to-day we took
From the gently flowing brook;
And above you they are spread
As on the silvery minnow's bed.
Here we also leave you food;
For it is a weary road
You again must travel o'er
Ere you reach the happy shore."

This said, the radiant vision fair
Vanished quickly into air.

THE TWO BROTHERS.

And then two youths of gentle mien
Went gliding by me o'er the green,
Who so great beauty had, and grace,
And loveliness in form and face,
That (as I had not long before
Been glancing into ancient lore)
I thought of Æneas goddess born!
How he, when cast away, forlorn,
Upon the Carthagenian strand
Did first before Queen Dido stand,
Delivered from the misty cloud
That hid him from the busy crowd, —
How beauty sparkled in his eyes,
Beauty descended from the skies!
The goddess curled his flowing hair;
Gave him youthful vigor rare;
Crowned his brow with ambient light;
Made his face serenely bright,
Like polished ivory beauteous bold,
Or Parian marble gemmed with gold.
I thought of fair Apollo, too,
With his far-shooting silver bow,
And golden quiver, glittering bright,
And arrows dipped in healing light, —
God of benevolence and truth;
The god of beauty and of youth —

Immortal, glorious, fearless, young —
Sweet his heavenly lyre rung;
The soul of harmony he fired;
The silent Muses he inspired.
Would thou, my Muse, by him were taught,
Had spark of heavenly fire caught,
Like sirens on the lonely isle,
To charm the passer-by awhile,
That he might lend attentive ear
This story from thy lips to hear —
(Of no imaginary act,
But well-authenticated fact)
Of love two youths each other bore —
So great as seldom known before!
They brothers were, and they were *men;*
And true they were not "white;" but then
'T is not the color of the skin
That tells us of the heart within.
They lived together; hunted game;
And, beside, they thought of *fame.*
However much men in their talk,
The love of glory seem to mock,
Should they the truth in candor own,
Would gladly have their own names known;
For 't is a feeling, and confest,
Which dwells in almost every breast
From that of humblest of the earth
To those of highest rank and birth.
And God himself — Ancient of Days! —
Commands that men shall sing his praise.

3

Who would not, like the Condor, seek
To gain the Andes' loftiest peak,
Could he thence on wings arise,
And soar toward the azure skies
And pass pale Cynthia in his flight,
And on the morning star alight,
And there amid effulgence dwell
For longer time than tongue can tell?
No labors are for man too hard
Where renown is the reward;
For this did Raphael command
The pencil with untiring hand;
For this Beethoven, deaf and old,
Unwrapped sweet music's every fold;
For this blind Milton sought in song,
And toiled so deep, and toiled so long!
The love of praise raised up, we know,
Demosthenes and Cicero;
'T was this that fashioned the "Greek Slave;"
'T was this made Bonaparte so brave.
Among Red Men the surest way
To honor, is the foe to slay;
Him they call supremely great
Who can most martial deeds relate.
The brothers, then, we cannot blame
For feeding the heroic flame.
The elder, chasing deer one day
Beyond the prairies, far away,
Came where the hunting ground he saw
Of the long hated Dakota;
Before his mind rose every one

Of all the wrongs that had been done
By that dread people to his own, —
(His aged father they had slain,
Whilst he was passing o'er the plain,
And ere they let his soul depart,
Tore from his breast his bleeding heart,
And, fiend-like, laughed to see it pant, —
On high they flung it for a taunt!)
Could he restrain his raging ire, —
From his veins expel the fire, —
As appeared distinct in view
One that seemed the savage Sioux?
"Be true," said he, "my trusty bow,
Lay the abhorred villain low!"
And then an arrow keen he took;
With flint 't was pointed from the brook;
And feathered from the eagle's wing;
And bound around with sinew string.
The bow he drew with mighty force;
The dart went hissing on its course,
Unseen, so swift it winged the air;
He saw it seek the bosom bare;
And, though afar it then had sped,
He saw the blood come gushing red.
The victim threw his hands on high
And sunk upon the turf to die;
The victor made exulting shout —
A foe was slain he had no doubt.
O youth, what fate must thee attend,
Should it not prove a foe; but *friend?*
Now with an eager haste he ran,
And stood above the dying man,

And stooping down, the scalp to take,
(A trophy for his honor's sake,)
When lo, instead of hated *Sioux*,
The friendly *Iowa* he knew!
He paused: the knife fell to the ground;
He drew the arrow from the wound.
Like the stern commander bold
Who by the messenger is told,
" The city of deserved hate
Will on no terms capitulate;
But dare unto the latest hour
With deadly scorn defy his power."
Anger rushes to his face;
He cries aloud, " The mortars place;
For she shall yield in dire disgrace!"
Ten thousand comets, as it were,
Soon are flaming in the air,
As if their course had wrathful fled
To descend upon her head!
Death and Destruction reign around;
And mighty Ruin strews the ground!
Behold! her gates she opens wide;
The hero enters them in pride!
His plume is waving in the wind;
His soldiers follow him behind;
High he holds his peerless head;
Beneath his feet he spurns the dead;
Until he finds — now free from pain —
A lovely lady 'mong the slain —
Sweetly wrapped in death — at rest —
A smiling infant on her breast.

Behold the hero bowing low!
Adown his check the warm tears flow!
He takes the babe upon his arm,
And saves the innocent from harm.
And so the youth; how his heart bled!
How fain would he have raised the dead!
Alas! he finds his grief too late;
So firm are the decrees of fate!
Before those eyes a darkness rose;
The spirit sought a long repose.
Awhile he stands in mute suspense;
Then with a tender eloquence: —
" And thou hast found the spirit land,
Sent by an undesigning hand;
My hopes with thine are at an end;
For this my death must make amend."
And then his way he homeward bent,
Soliloquizing as he went: —
" ' No, he did it purposely,
And to escape doth falsify.'
Thus will they answer my defense,
When I avow my innocence
Of having murdered by design.
I plainly see what fate is mine,
And to the same myself resign."
Some months had passed, when men were sent
Him to demand for punishment;
And they found him on his bed;
Disease had humbled low his head;
Yet willing was, at their command,
To rise and seek the foreign land;

And their unfeeling orders were,
" By coming morn he should prepare
With them to go upon the way ;
Or ill or well, he must obey."

THE INDIAN VILLAGE.

A lovely " Iowa " village stood
Within the shadow of a wood,
And by the margin of a stream ;
How happy did its people seem !
Around the council-house behold
A great concourse of young and old !
Is not the purpose of the throng
The avenging of a wrong ?
And was the youth torn from his bed,
And here before accusers led ?
A youth of humble modesty
Within the council-house we see ;
Such beauty brightening in his face
As would well an angel grace ;
Reclining lowly on the ground,
While chiefs and braves, with look profound,
Are seated in a circle round.
Behold the leading chief arise !
Now on the youth he rests his eyes,
And thus he speaks in accents slow : —
" Ere this the just avenging blow
Deep in the dust had laid you low ;
But ancient custom of our land,
Bids that you first before us stand,

With privilege of self-defense,
With all you have of eloquence."
And so, the youth rose from the ground,
And cast a pleasant look around ;
Then from his robe freed his right arm,
And stood erect, nor in alarm.
All eyes surveyed the brave young man,
As with sweet accent he began : —

" Fathers ! I have my death-song sung ;
  With joy my voice its numbers rung ;
  For as I came along to die,
  I heard the honey-bee flit by ;
  Its course it turned toward the sky.
  Methought it spake my spirit so : —
' Arise, arise, from fields below
  To where the sweeter flowers blow !
  Their cups of bliss to thee no more
  Shall close upon the happy shore.'
  Wherefore grim Death, then, should I fear ?
  My own free choice doth bring me here !
  It is not, Fathers ! my desire
  That words shall mitigate your ire ;
  The tom'hawk on my head must fall ;
  Nor this may I injustice call ;
  It would not now the stroke prevent
  To claim my brother innocent
  Of having with vile purpose slain
  One of your braves upon the plain.
  Fathers ! here I take the place
  Of him whom you would now disgrace ;
  Into your hands my life I give ;
  O, that my brother long may live !

Upon his bed he lies, too ill
Himself your mandate to fulfill!
I came without his own consent,
And much he strove me to prevent;
Such has his kindness to me been,
Would I ɴoᴛ die for him, 't were sin."

Thus having said, again he sate
Him down among these men of state,
And there awaited calm his fate.
Did they arise with furious yell,
Bend over him like fiends of hell,
Bury the tom'hawk in his brain,
And bid him sleep, nor wake again?
Ah no, full glad am I to say
How well they welcomed him that day!
They freely gave the friendly hand,
And bade him with the bravest stand;
And then resolved to make a feast
In honor of the worthy guest!
So, down into the glen they go,
Hard by the rivulet below, —
I trow, no fairer spot of ground
In all the boundless West is found!
Dame Nature there has carpet spread,
And giant oaks nod overhead;
'Neath craggy rock is sylvan spring,
Near which by moonlight maidens sing;
Nor distant hence afar is found
A spacious grot beneath the ground,
Where oft young men and maids repair,
And presents in their hands they bear

For the good spirit that dwells there.
Then as the dusky eve draws nigh,
They seek a mossy seat hard by,
Where they may catch the lovely sound
Of water as it tinkles down
From a shelving rock above ;
Here they sit and talk of love ;
And oftentimes prolong their stay
While Hesperus crowns departing day,
And after she has long sought rest
On her couch low in the west.
A deep-worn circle, too, is seen,
Near by the spring, upon the green,
Where now young braves are chanting loud
And aged warriors, bold and proud —
(All painted o'er with many a hue ;
And each a hieroglyphic true —
Telling of the foes they slew)
Are dancing many an antic round,
To rudest instrumental sound ;
Waving the war-club oft on high
Or pointing arrows to the sky,
Portraying how they battles gained,
Or how the bison's blood they drained,
Or how the bow, from crag on high,
Brought down the eagle bold to die.
All the village throng is there, —
The young, the old, the brave, the fair,
So that now under every tree
A group there is in gladsome glee !
Participating in the sport,
Their guest is happy as at court !

Meanwhile are matrons hurrying fast
To prepare the rich repast.
Soon, at a well-known signal, all,
Male and female, great and small,
Place themselves in order round,
Low seated on the grassy ground;
While those that are of high degree
On elevated mound we see —
A place of greater dignity —
And honored far above the rest,
We may behold the youthful guest.
To him they first refreshment bring,
And then to others of the ring
Promiscuously, till soon 't is known
That well supplied is every one;
When with great joy they all partake
Of bounteous gift of wood and lake;
Of maize-bread, product of the soil;
But most of fruit of huntsman's toil, —
The flesh of buffalo and bear;
Of the elk and of the deer;
And fish — the pike and salmon rare —
All that fair Nature here affords
Graces this banquet of her lords;
Much of the fruit of vine and tree
And honey of the working bee.
How sweet a nectar, too, they bring
From the ever-bubbling spring!
Bubbling from the sands below —
Sands as pure and white as snow!
How happy was the feast, and long;
And echoed oft the hills with song —

Song of welcome to the stranger —
Welcome there, all free from danger!

A SONG OF WELCOME.

Welcome, stranger, welcome here!
Thou art welcome to our cheer!

Has he not a loving brother,
　And may be a sister dear,
And an old heart-broken mother,
　And an aged father near,
Who are now bowed down in sorrow
　For this loved one good and brave,
Fearing lest the coming morrow
　Find him slumbering in the grave?

Do not think our eyes so blinded;
　Do not think our souls so vile;
Do not think us so dark minded;
　Do not think us lost in guile,
That we cannot see, all glowing!
　Light — a spark from God above!
Or seeing, and its purpose knowing,
　Would stifle such a light of love!

Welcome, stranger, welcome here!
Thou art worthy of our cheer!

The sun his face began to hide
Within the vast Pacific tide,

Ere they the village reach again,
Where all seek rest save the young men;
They on their coursers prance afar
While lingers the bright evening star.
It was indeed a lovely sight
To look upon them by moonlight,
Riding through woods and over plains —
Without saddle, without reins!
Now all meeting in one place,
Loud neigh the horses for the race;
The riders bending forward then,
Their coursers (more than ten times ten)
Spring onward with a mighty bound;
The prairies tremble far around!
And thundering hoofs on air resound.
They speed, they speed full fast away!
But see two steeds of glossy bay —
How sweet the moonbeams on them play'
They leave the others far behind —
Much like the Anglo-Saxon mind
In great achievements for mankind.

The night is past, bright morning glows;
And all have had a calm repose;
And they have said their fervent prayers
To Him who ever for them cares, —
(To whom devotedly they pray,
At morn and eve of every day).
Now, ere the stranger guest depart,
They show again a kindly heart,
By making presents to him there

Which he may with his brother share:
Two good suits of hunters' clothes,
Two wampum belts, and two strong bows;
Then many of their dearest beads;
And last, the pair of bright bay steeds,
Which on the happy eve before
In the race had triumph bore!

He, joyful, went to greet his brother;
Long they lived to love each other.

THE CONCLUSION.

And now, fair stream, have I mused long,
And lengthened out a thankless song!
It is thy fault, sweet stream, I say,
That I have wandered so away!
Why do the lovely sunbeams lave
And glisten in thy rippling wave?
Why do the willows on thy brink
Bow down their heads and seem to drink?
Why does the pretty "silver-side"
Play through thy waters so in pride?
Had never these my vision crossed
Perhaps I had not now been lost!
Why is that venerable mound
Upon thy level margin found?
Who made it thus of earth and stone
To thee, O ancient stream, 't is known!
I look upon it, and my mind
In thought no resting-place can find;

I think that it, perhaps, was built
Where blood, a deluge, had been spilt;
Perhaps, beneath where it arose
Bones of a patriot repose;
While this alone by it is told, —
"*A people dwelt here once of old;*"
And seems to mention with the same, —
"*They dwelt here ere the Indian came.*"
The Indian! Keokuk the great!
Pride of a patriotic State!
In battle, braver ne'er was one;
In wisdom, the bright noonday sun;
In eloquence, a crownéd king, —
Surpassed by none in any thing
That can exalt a Red Man's name
And give to him undying fame!
No power so strong — no base-born bribe —
Could lead him to betray his tribe.
Be ye reproved, vile statesmen old,
Who love your country less than gold!
"*I liked my towns, — my corn-fields, too:
For these, O white man, I fought you!*"
Thus speaks the wrongéd Indian dead;
'T was thus the patriot Black Hawk said.
Be long, my lovely Iowa, be
Home of as noble-hearted free!

Thou stream, farewell! I shall be lorn
Till smiling dawns another morn,
When here I once again may stray
And while an happy hour away!

June, 1858.

IOWA.

———◆———

PART SECOND

THE PRESENT.

A MORNING'S MEDITATION ON THE BANKS OF THE DES MOINES.

"Let all the ends thou aimest at be thy country's,
Thy God's, and truth's."
                                            SHAKSPEARE.

I NOW the wished-for morn behold ;
The Sun displays his crown of gold ;
But many smiling days have flown,
The dove hath uttered many a moan,
Since I, reclining here alone,
Mused in melancholy mood,
As the sorrowful Past I viewed.
Let my thoughts this morning be
From all melancholy free ;
Indeed, the Present gives my mind,
Of images a pleasing kind ;
And the Future meets my view
Illumined with a golden hue.

Are not these Western streams as fair
As Tiber, Thames, the Seine, or Ayr,
Danube, Vistula, Guadalquivir,
Or any European river ?

If e'en to Asia I should go,
And there behold the Hoang-ho,
Euphrates, Indus, Irawaddy,
Bramapootra, and Cambodia;
And stray through Africa awhile —
Behold the Niger and the Nile —
When from my wanderings I come
And view again the streams at home,
I ask, would these not seem to me
As fair as those beyond the sea?
Iowa, virgin State, is seen
Arrayed now in her robes of green —
A maid of more than mortal charms —
Diana in two happy arms,
As if from high come down again
To fair Endymion of men.
The river on her eastern side
Exalts my patriotic pride!
It needs no sounding trump of fame
To send abroad the well-known name.
The British bard would glad depart
From the monotony of Art,
Displayed before him all the while
Upon his much-loved native Isle,
Where hedges white in May, as snow,
Checker the land where'er he go, —
The flowery scene is fair, I know;
But Nature, wild and primitive,
There no longer seems to live.
Right glad would he depart, I say,
On Mississippi's banks to stray.

Along young Iowa's western side
Flows the Missouri deep and wide, —
Rivers beautiful and great
Are the pride of any State ;
And who will question this so true,
That Iowa hath not a few ?
Hers are the great and little Sioux,
The Turkey and Makoqueta,
Red Cedar, and the Iowa,
Besides " wide-bottomed " Chicaqua, —
Asipala (or swift Raccoon)
And many more, with which the Doon
And the far-renownéd Ayr
In length nor beauty can compare.
But for good reason have I passed
By thee, Des Moines, to name thee last :
However distant I may roam,
I find no place I love like home ;
And towns and cities I have seen
Exceeding beautiful, I ween,
But I prefer my village still,
Which I behold on yon green hill ;
Her damsels seem to me more fair
Than those I ever meet elsewhere.
For some good reason do I love
More than all others this my grove ;
High on yon bending hickory
The squirrel often speaks to me ;
Here on an evening calm and still
I hear the lonely whip-poor-will ;
While frequently I all day long

4

Sit listening to continual song, —
A choir chanting in this wood
A chorus to the praise of God,
Who hath sent Winter far away
And ushered in the vernal May.
All creatures seem thus to rejoice,
Without but one discordant voice.
From beak of little warbling bird
Hath any person ever heard,
(Although his locks be white with years)
" This world is but a vale of tears ? "
No, no, its little speech is this : —
" Behold our world, a world of bliss! "
It is indeed a very shame ;
It is blaspheming God's high name,
Who built the starry dome above,
Who filled the universe with love,
Crowned Beauty as a queen to reign
O'er all His glorious domain,
That any creature can be heard
To contradict the little bird !
Yes, the happy warblers sing
To welcome in the days of Spring —
And what a merry, merry lay!
How it delights my mind to-day
While on these pleasant banks I stray!
Ah, Des Moines, need I now tell,
Why 't is I like thy shores so well ?

Once musing on thy banks, O stream,
had a memorable dream ;

A beauteous maid before me stood;
She seemed a huntress of the wood;
And I beheld her bow unstrung;
Her quiver o'er her shoulder hung;
I saw not e'en an arrow there;
Around it wantoned her long hair;
Her dress seemed loosely o'er her placed,
Except 't was girdled round her waist;
Nor shoes had she upon her feet;
Her eyes so bright knew not deceit;
A lovely wreath of flowers hung
Around her neck; and them she flung,
With kindly smile, about my own;
Then meekly on a mossy stone
She sat her down, but not alone; —
It did not seem to wound her pride
That I should seat me by her side;
But now she looks on me in love;
She seems an angel from above!
Ah, now she passes from my view, —
Glides swiftly in a bark canoe,
Toward thy northern shores, fair stream;
And much I sorrow in my dream!
I see thy sparkling waves full plain;
She dips her paddle in again;
The trees behold the swift canoe,
And wave to her a kind adieu;
The birds now chant a mournful lay,
That she must pass from them away;
The woods and prairies grieve full sore,
That they shall see her face no more; —

Her every movement seems to tell,
In beauty none can her excel;
And what a voice was hers — so clear!
Methinks its accents now I hear
While she glides gracefully along,
Still caroling her farewell song.

FAREWELL SONG OF PRIMITIVE NATURE.

The Sun shall continue in his kindly duty
    Through days without number to come,
Of rising and painting this landscape with beauty,
    Then gliding with joy to his home.

And oft will he pass by the twelve constellations
    That encircle the heavens above ;
And Spring shall respond to his kind invitations,
    And be seen here as oft in her love.

The beautiful Summer, and Autumn fruit-laden,
    And white-bearded Winter severe,
Will return like a youth at the beck of a maiden,
    Whene'er he shall bid them appear.

Sable Night, as if wrapped in a robe of deep
        mourning,
    Will stalk here in sadness and gloom,
Till the moon shall arise with her silver adorn-
        ing,
    Like a spirit goes up from the tomb.

The stars gladly join her with beauty refulgent,
  Like eyes when they sparkle with mirth;
Thick clouds are all banished; for winds were
      indulgent, —
  Behold now a glorious earth!

I leave this loved land; but I go not in sorrow:
  I bid now adieu to this shore;
My sister comes after to dwell here to-mor-
      row, —
  Sweet land, shall I see thee no more?

The storm-cloud shall rise from the West with
      its thunder
  Deep-echoing terror afar;
The three-forkéd lightning shall cleave oaks asun-
      der, —
  Dread shaft from a furious star.

When these plains are uplifted by volcanic fires
  That sleep now in quiet below,
And pierce the high clouds with the rock-pointed
      spires
  Encased in perpetual snow;

When these rivers have fled and are lost in the
      ocean;
  Nor their trace can we longer discern;
And all things are changed in the mighty com-
      motion,
  Behold once again I return!

As this one vanishes from sight
Behold another vision bright!
Another maid approaching me, —
Hers is the voice of " Liberty."

A SONG OF "LIBERTY."

Nature and I twin sisters are,
  We love alike the wilderness;
But still we wander oft afar,
  And give to Art her mightiness

'T is I the souls of men inspire
  With longings for immortal fame;
I kindle in their breasts the fire;
  I fan it to a mounting flame.

Cast but a glance at ancient Greece;
  Whose strength exalted her so high?
In war the mightiest; in peace
  She seems uplifted to the sky!

'T was Liberty gave her her men;
  Her men created her renown;
But can I not call up again
  As great as wore the olive crown?

Another age, another clime,
  Where Tyranny ne'er drew a breath,
May yet behold a scene sublime, —
  The mighty, as though raised from death.

Raised freed as from their former clay, —
   Debasing passions laid aside, —
Raised to enjoy a full-orbed day,
   And feel a more becoming pride.

Protected by the one true God
   Whom they with reverence behold;
They 'll walk in paths before untrod,
   And darkest mysteries unfold.

This lovely land they 'll re-create, —
   Make Eden bloom on earth once more;
Here, here will build a noble State,
   Greater than Attica of yore.

Will any lift the ruthless hand;
   By any will that stroke be given,
Shall drive me from this beauteous land? —
   He drives me back for aye to Heaven!

No, lovely being! much I pray
That none may banish thee away;
For well I know how man is blest
Whilst thou continuest his guest.
I would, O Liberty, that he
Might bow to earth and worship thee;
I would thy temples here might rise
On marble columns to the skies;
I would have thee adored as one
Next to Jehovah and his Son.
Young men, and maidens, let us raise

To her a daily hymn of praise!
Des Moines, upon thy verdant shore
May she continue evermore!
May never gaze on thee, that thing —
The curse of human-kind — a king;
May never look upon thy wave,
While time shall last, a trembling slave!
Upon thy northern wave the Sioux
Is paddling still his birch canoe.
What lovely prospect meets my view! —
The rolling prairies, like a sea
In vast and wild sublimity,
There lie with an unbroken sod,
Untilled but by the hand of God;
He sows the seeds of grass and flowers;
He moistens them with vernal showers.
But look abroad in summer-time;
I'm sure in England's foggy clime,
With all the aid that Art affords,
With all the efforts of rich lords,
A garden blooming half so fair
Never yet has flourished there.
What are her parks, to one who here
Has chased the bison, elk, and deer,
O'er pathless plains, and through wild woods,
And wandered in those solitudes,
Where could be heard no grating sound
Of mill, nor cattle lowing round,
Nor crowing cock, nor yelping hound,
Nor sportman's gun, nor tolling bell,
The charms of Nature to dispel, —

Has watched the beaver build like men,
And killed the wild duck and marsh hen;
Caught wolves and badgers, lynx, raccoon,
And shot on Spirit Lake the loon?
Ah, Spirit Lake! she is to-day
As beautiful as Loch-Achray!
'T is true, the "Minstrel" here can view
No lofty rocks, no Ben-venue;
Here Nature doffs her awful charms;—
Holds out to him her lovely arms.
I mount on Fancy's wings the air;
I seek a woody island, where
Upon a grassy couch reclined,
Fond recollections throng my mind,
Of happy days, when but a child,
I glided o'er such waters wild,
And, glad, on every danger smiled.
The little boat my father guides;
My playful hands hang o'er its sides,
And dabble in the foaming waves,
That rise like spectres from the graves,—
I do not know their rage to fear;
Their music joyfully strikes mine ear.
'T is thus I yet on life's waves ride,
By no wild breakers terrified;
I let them roll unheeded by,
Nor seem to know the danger nigh,—
Content and hope fill up my breast,
And threat what will, I still am blest!
Protected by a Father's care,
Approach not fear; away despair!

The raging winds have sought their caves,
And now subsided are the waves;
Not e'en a rush is seen to shake;
So smooth the surface of the lake,
I see the fishes at their play;
I see them quickly dart away.
What dreadful form to them appears,
That now so mightily wakes their fears? —
A giant monster, moving slow,
And dips two frightful fins below.
Thus men take fright ofttimes as great
At monsters their own fears create;
Church-yards by night swarm with grim
          ghosts,
Dark Hades has dire fiends by hosts,
And Pluto reigns supreme o'er all
That dwell within the horrid wall.
We now pass round a point of land
Where branching cedars thickly stand;
Wild berries, plums, and grapes abound,
And nuts of many kinds are found.
But what a lovely prospect lies
Outspread before my gladdened eyes!
The lake with boats is dotted o'er
From yon small village on the shore;
The fisherman sinks down his seine
And rows toward that shore again;
And the light anchors others weigh
Who have been angling all the day,
And homeward turn, because the sun
His daily course has well-nigh run;

While each loud sound the paddles make
Is borne by Echo o'er the lake,
And her sweet voice is plainly heard
To answer each loud-spoken word.
But hark! what tender sound I hear,
That strikes so mournfully mine ear!
'T is borne on Zephyr's wings from far, —
The music of a soft guitar.

ADIEU.

I love my country's maidens,
   Wherever I may roam ;
But those that are most dear to me
   Are of my village home ;

Because I love that village ;
   I love her hills around ;
Her woods and her wild prairies ;
   Her streamlets' murmuring sound.

There comes a voice unbidden,
   Nor can I tell thee why,
Commanding me to love my home, —
   That voice is from on high.

While I have been a stranger,
   Far from that home away,
There never has unkindness yet
   Beclouded my fair day.

No maid has e'er despised me,
　Although of high degree;
Nor has she ever spurned me
　From her sweet company.

Must the tear of bitter grief
　Now first be made to start;
Must the heaviest stroke be given
　Against my feeling heart,

By those I prize so highly
　Of my own village home,
By those I prize more highly far
　Than wealth of ancient Rome?

But now I am determined,
　Ah! never more to feel
Such cruel wound upon my heart,
　Worse than a wound of steel!

So, in the happy woods I'll seat
　Me on a mossy stone;
I'll strike upon my sounding harp
　And leave the maids alone!

Dame Nature, I shall woo her
　With all my words of love;
I'll woo the flowers of the ground
　'll woo the birds above;

I 'll woo the gentle sunset;
  I 'll woo the evening breeze,
While it sings on joyful wings
  Among my forest trees!

A large and handsome boat I see;
It bears a happy company,
That came to spend a joyful day
Upon this little cape in play, —
Gathering fruits, and wreathing flowers;
Reclining 'neath the shady bowers
Formed by Nature's sylvan fingers,
Where, a wood-nymph, still she lingers,
Plucking water-lilies fair
To adorn her raven hair;
Holding in her lovely hand
A branch of cedar for a wand;
Protecting all the living things
That walk the earth, or fly on wings;
Directing the industrious bees
To take for mansions her tall trees;
Painting the wings of butterflies
With colors, like the evening skies.
To-day, beneath her shades so cool,
Those of a Christian Sabbath-school
Sat down and drank of happiness, —
Drank from the cup of social bliss;
But now at evening they forsake
The grove and sail upon the lake.
As towards their homes they haste along,
All are joined in sacred song.

A PSALM OF DAVID.*

Oh, now let us sing to the Lord a new song,
  For marvelous deeds hath He done ;
With His holy arm and right hand ever strong
  He hath the great victory won.

By love hath He conquered, salvation made known,
  And now may the heathen rejoice, —
To them is His righteousness openly shown ;
  They hear His kind welcoming voice.

How well He remembered in mercy and truth
  To smile upon Israel, too ;
The ends of the earth, — all the aged and youth, —
  Are led His salvation to view.

Let all the wide world to Him joyfully raise
  A noise of thanksgiving on high ;
With the voice of a psalm on the harp, sing His
    praise, —
  Sing praise unto Him who is nigh.

With trumpets and sound of the glad cornet make
  A joyful noise to our King ;
Let seas loudly roar, and their creatures awake,
  And the world, and all in it, sing.

Let floods clap their hands ; let the gladsome hills
    smile
  Before Him who bade them have birth ;

* Psalm xcviii.

He cometh, and they shall behold Him erewhile
  With righteousness judging the earth !

But now I leave this lake's wild shore,
Perhaps to visit it no more.
Iowa — thirteen years a State,*
And now appears among the great!
Let her proud banner be unfurled
And borne in triumph round the world!
"Oh, I have found the beauteous one, —
The fairest land beneath the sun!"
Thus strangers, when they first behold
This land more bright than glittering gold;
Thus speak they when their eyes first greet
Her plains, like boundless fields of wheat;
When first her vast green forests rise
Conspicuous before their eyes;
When first they see her rivers roll
Through fields exhaustless of rich coal;
When first her marble beds appear;
When to her lime-stone quarries near;
When they her mines of lead explore;
When they behold her iron ore
And copper on the river shore,
And fire-clay and quartzite sand,
And gypsum underneath the land.
Thus is she great in mineral worth;
She is the garden of the earth!
How very wise in all her laws!
How glorious in Freedom's cause!

* Admitted into the Union Dec. 28, 1846.

On the Escutcheon give her far
The broadest stripe, the brightest star!
Escutcheon of the thirty-three, —
The coat-of-arms of Liberty,
And of a noble family!
Yes, Iowa indeed is fair;
Of streams of water has her share;
Is rich in minerals; and her soil
Will bless for aye the plowman's toil.
Who o'er the prairies looks abroad,
And does not see the hand of God
Preparing them through ages past
To be the homes of men who cast
The seed abroad, and reap again
A rich reward in golden grain!
Who has prophetic ken to tell
How many millions here may dwell;
What mighty deeds will here be done;
What wreaths of laurel here be won!
What men appear whose names shall stand
An honor to their native land!

May, 1859.

PASTORALS OF THE PRAIRIES.

PASTORALS OF THE PRAIRIES.

THEOCRITUS, how sweet thy pastoral
    strains !
    " Where were ye, nymphs, in what
      sequestered grove ;
    Where were ye, nymphs, when Daphnis
      pined for love ? "
For love have died unnumbered shepherd swains ;
O'er all the world her sway Love still maintains ;
    For her fair brow, of flowers are garlands
      wove ;
    Through woods disconsolate her votaries
      rove ; —
The wild rose blooms upon these western plains ;
My lovely Jane 's the lily and wild rose,
    The prairie-lily and blue violet ;
Upon her cheeks their beauties all repose.
    Apollo paints the evening clouds, and yet
Their hues are not as beautiful as those
That modestly her heart of love disclose.

II.

Why did you, when we parted last, dear Jane,
        Bow down your head as if you were in
            grief?
        I deem you were, and can I give relief?
Say, do you fear that I may not remain
True to you, love? Oh, think it not again!
        Why, dearest, I am not an Autumn leaf!
        You whispered, though my love to you be
            brief,
Still yours in life would never, never wane,
And that it would far hence in Heaven be bright,
        When you are called to live with angels
            there.
Jane, Jane, you are my heart's chiefest delight;
        " Thou art to me the fairest of the fair;"
I love you, yes, *I love you*, and for aye;
My love will brighten to the "perfect day."

III.

The pretty lock of your long hair you gave
        To me, Jane, I will preserve forever!
        No sweet relic have I of my mother,
My sainted mother, (she's been in her grave
Twelve years now,) no sweet relic save
        A lock of her dark hair, and mem'ry of her
        Prayers and many tears. Jennie, I prefer
This dear relic 'bove all rubies; a slave
To vice can I become and look upon it?

Her words and thine, so kind, are near my
  heart;
Their hallowed influence can ne'er depart;
Her love and thine—immortal, though the sonnet
  That speaks these praises perish in a day;
  For so our fondest labors pass away.

IV.

Now from my eye there falls the gushing tear;
  Oh that I now were seated by thy side,
  My lovely Jane, of no disdainful pride!
Oh come, and let me whisper in thy ear
Kind words that are not for the world to hear!
  And, whispering, press so tenderly thy
  cheek.
  Sweet Jennie, ever loving, ever meek,
I worship thee, my only, only dear!
The livelong night I'd sit embracing thee, —
  The silvery moon, so chaste and fair, alone
Might look upon us. Yes, Diana, we
  Would have thy company; for thou hast
  shone
On lovers many a year. Thy sovereignty
  We would obey; for love thou, too, hast
  known.

V.

Again I kiss these lovely locks of hair! —
  Which love I best, my mother's, Jane, or
  thine?

I cannot tell; let them together twine!
My love I'll equally between them share;
To love them thus I never can forbear;
    Deep in my heart behold I them enshrine!
    My mother loved me; Jennie now is mine!
Her loving heart, — Oh what a heart! Is there
In Heaven a holier fount of love? The fount
    That flows from 'neath the throne of God —
    a throne
Of gold, high up upon the Holy Mount!
    On earth a purer spring cannot be shown, —
While here I live, still may I taste her love,
And then throughout eternity above!

VI.

O Jane, that I could be with you to-day! —
    This Autumn day; wild plums and grapes
    for thee
    I'd pluck from off the bush and vine;
    and we
Beneath the towering trees afar would stray,
As we did oft in the pleasant Summer gone.
    Now we would sit upon a log o'ergrown
    With moss, and listening to the sorrowful
    moan
Of Autumn winds, I'd read Anacreon
To thee again; — no, I'd Tibulus read, —
    Some mournful elegy of Delia's scorn, —
    Of unrequited love. Oh, how forlorn
Was that young man! I'm thankful that I'm
    freed

From such as Delia was. My Jane will
    ne'er
By cruelty cause me a single tear.

VII.

Is that not, Jane, a pretty landscape, say?
    The lowland there extending to the west, —
    A lovely, fertile plain that now is dressed
In garment of ripe maize; — and see, away
Beyond the Des Moines stream, the hills so fair!
    As soon as night shall come flames may
        appear
    Upon their tops, darting like frighted deer,
Leaving the prairies wild all black and bare!
When Spring returns, how soon the tender grass
    And pretty flowers again we see. The rose
    And violet and lily then disclose
Their beauty. I remember now, alas!
    Those dear love-tokens I received from thee,
    Some person wickedly has stolen from me.

VIII.

A lovely damsel loved an humble swain, —
    (Truly a comely maid in mind and mien;
    One of more modesty was never seen; —
To tell the truth, it is my darling Jane!
He that's beloved by her need not complain;
    She is the sun most glorious in its sheen;
    On whom it shines, his days must pass
        serene;

He never need to shed a tear again.)
And she (that he 'd conject' whose was her heart)
      Placed in his Book two lovely roses red,
And two blue violets. He would not part
      With them for all the gold of earth, he said,
And so he felt; but they were stolen away;
      Yet he believes her love will not decay.

IX.

Do you remember, Jane, the little wren
      That built her nest so near your door last
      Spring?
      Her pretty mate, — you 've listened to him
      sing, —
From morn till eve he 'd sing; nor cease, but when
The rain came down in torrents; and if then
      A moment, 't was to shake his dripping
      wing:
      Raising his beak toward Heaven his notes
      now ring
Clearer than ever, — thinks of love again!
Thus stays he by his spouse through sun and
      shower,
      And sings to her in tender, loving strains,
Gladdening her heart through every passing hour.
      Jane, I 'll continue 'mongst the truest
      swains;
Just like that bird I 'll sing by thy sweet bower;
      Forsake thee not, long as my life remains!
September, 1860.

SATIRICAL POEMS.

M. ARATHUSA ALLEN: — I am persuaded that, if there is worth in any of my poems, these entitled PRIDE and FASHION merit consideration. In them I battle against wrong. My *ensign* is *Truth;* my guide is the *Word of God* and the sayings of the wise and good; and that which impels me forward is *love of my native country.*

I would associate with your name these especially, that they may be, the more worthily, preserved and read. You are blessed with abundant wealth, and you possess what is of greater value, — a heart sensitive to the wants of the poor; and you are only proud in the consciousness of having performed noble actions. You esteem " good works," your bright adornment, above all ornaments of " gold or pearls or 'broidered hair." " After this manner, in the olden time, the holy women also, who trusted in God, adorned themselves."

LEONARD BROWN.

PRIDE.

PART I.

"The poor have the Gospel preached to them."

O preach the gospel to a dying world,
How high the calling; what a glorious
work !
To go about, like Jesus, doing good, —
Preaching glad tidings to the poor. " The rich
Can scarcely enter Heaven," the Bible says.
The heavens will pass away; the earth will melt
With fervent heat, and yet the Truth remain.
The rich hate God, — are enemies of Christ;
They shake their bags of gold at Him and laugh.
They *buy* His ministers, — His ministers?
The "wolves dressed in sheep's clothing," — these
they buy;
And murder those that yield not to their bidding.
Who shot and hung devoted men of God,
Because they dared to cry aloud and say,
That slavery is accursed of Him, and wrong?

The proud, the rich in this world's goods, — 'twas
    they ;
And they *bought up* a pack of hungry "wolves"
To advocate and call the wrong "divine."
Just so it is to-day, right in our midst ;
The rich are as intolerant as Hell !
The preacher must succumb to *pride*, or else
Be driven like a vagabond of earth ;
And soon he hath not where to lay his head ;
And like the Lord, betrayed and crucified,
He dies a blessed martyr to the truth.
" I send my wife to church," the merchant says,
" So finely dressed, my silks to advertise."
" I keep a rented pew to show my furs,"
Another says, "and thus I gain big sales."
The church is but a show-case of fine goods, —
A mighty Barnum-advertising shop.

PART II.

A PETITION.

Here in Thy house this Sabbath-day
Thy followers have met to pray;
My Saviour, they have barred the door
Against the lowly and the poor.

The rich alone, in silk and lace,
The house of God may fitly grace;
So fine are they, that (to be sure)
They look with scorn upon the poor.

A mother came, not long ago,
To the house of prayer in calico, —
(The finest dress she had she wore,)
She felt abashed for being poor.

For Satan wanders far and wide
In guise of Fashion and of Pride, —
He in this church hath shut the door
Against the lowly and the poor.

And Christ is spit upon with scorn,
For He was in a manger born ; —
Up Calvary the cross He bore
To save the lowly and the poor.

Sweet Saviour, take me in Thy care,
And answer this my fervent prayer, —
That ministers, for Thee, once more
May preach the gospel to the poor.

. . . .

If my Pegasus now begins to flag,
  Perhaps the creature needs a little fodder;
He 's certainly a very awkward nag, —
  There never was a pony any odder, —
Is young, — has never travelled much to brag, —
  His pinions, too, are only yet a rod or
So long; — yet I 'm in good hopes that soon
He 'll mount aloft and soar beyond the moon.

But first, I 'll ride the creature somewhat down-
      ward;
  Like Æneas, perhaps, we 'll enter Hell;
If not, I 'll urge upon him to go townward,
  Which will my purpose answer just as well;
But, then, I guess I 'd rather ride him mound-
      ward;
  Stir up the bones which in deep darkness dwell;
Stir up the bones; look on the skeletons
Of those who once were counted " pretty ones."

What of the dead? What of the mothers sleeping
  Low in the cold and solitary ground?
They are not there. But are they shadows weep-
      ing
  Among the many that the poet found —

(He whom Virgil guided) where those, lowly
    creeping,
  Bent down with burdens that their follies
    bound —
Bewailed that they had not sought higher pleas-
    ures
Than flow from pride, and seeking earthly treas-
    ures ?

What of the dead ? I ask again, what of them ?
  They lived, were human beings full of weak-
    ness ;
And yet no creature could be much above them ;
  (For Shakspeare tells the truth, if right I guess),
" How in action like an angel ! " (Love them !)
  " In apprehension like a god ! " (Goodness !)
Man is great ! (and he is little, too), —
More wonderful than are the worlds we view.

That he is great, behold an Isaac Newton ;
  The universe he held within his hand ;
For him a little plaything was the sun ;
  He weighed the planets as if grains of sand ;
He learned from God as I might learn from one
  Who is above me, but will near me stand, —
Who is above me, but alike in kind ;
So he with God, perhaps, had kindred mind.

He read the universe as 't were a poem ;
  The written music of the spheres he read ;
He read God's Illiad far beyond the proem ;
  He felt, — appreciated what it said, —

The mighty minds, a mighty mind can know
    them;
Who but a patriot *knows* why Warren bled?
Newton, long since, has entered Heaven's por-
    tal, —
Looks on God's face, and is, like Him, im-
    mortal!

   .   .   .   .   .   .

The crowning virtue of a city belle,
    Which gives to her her whole preëminence,
Is not (what it is *not* let me first tell) —
    Is not a head filled with superior sense;
Is not devotion to the image that fell
    Down from Jupiter, — but *impudence*, —
Impudence and Fashion walk hand-in-hand, —
Sin and Satan let loose in the land.

But I have faith in God and man and *woman;*
    He that speaks truth can never speak in vain, —
We all do err, because to err is human, —
    Who would not gladly see the Devil slain?
I take my saber now to fight that foeman,
    And I'll strike right and left with might and
    main, —
I do believe (I say it without passion)
Our greatest foe to-day is foreign *fashion.*

Our patriot ladies, give to them due credit;
    American women stand first in the world;
The giant Vice, they threaten to behead it;
    Their banners Amazonian are unfurled, —

The " mightier than the sword " they wield ; 't is
    said it
  Pierces through joints and marrow, when 't is
    hurled, —
'Gainst Slavery envenomed bolts they throw, —
Behold a heroine, — Harriet Beecher Stowe !

It may be wrong to hold a man in slavery, —
  To bind the clanking fetter on his heel
May be abstractly vilest kind of knavery ;
  The trembling slave may very badly feel.
But pause, ye fair ones, ere you show your
    bravery ;
  Consider ere you sharpen up your steel ;
Consider, and 't will end your bitter passion ;
Think, ladies, *Slavery in the South's the Fashion !*

Fashion in the South will flog a Negro ;
  Fashion in the North will kill a woman.
Both may be wrong, but which one is the
    " bigger "
  I cannot say ; they 're either quite inhuman.
At evil, North or South, will pull a trigger
  More quickly than I, perhaps but few men ;
But I will not a Northern sinner brag of, —
Turn round and shoot a Southern sinner's leg off.

And Fashion everywhere should be protected !
  " De gustibus non disputandem est," —
It is a thing that ought not be dissected ;
  There would n't seem much sense in it at best,

6

To one whose head is not with it affected, —
    We ought not pity, then, the slave distressed. .
How beautiful the Chinese lady's feet!
The flat head of an Indian, how neat!

What means, I ask, a Bloomer-dress convention?
    An effort to shake off a foreign yoke;
And certainly a laudable intention;
    With foreign yokes our necks are well-nigh
        broke.
My sympathy in that I need not mention, —
    However I am not prepared to croak
In favor of the costume that 's selected,
Until I have its modesty detected.

But I admire a " charming " style of dress, —
    The bright adornment of th' immortal mind;
For it is woman's highest loveliness, —
    To fit her for God's converse 't is designed.
Ah, see in Paradise bright Beatrice,
    Ever beloved and loveliest of her kind; --
Then clothe the mind and heart with heavenly
        graces;
They 'll brighter glow than rouge on pretty faces.

And I admire the patriotic notion
    Held by all ladies of superior mind, —
That foreign fashions ought not cross the ocean,
    Nor in this country any footing find.
My prayer is, they may set the ball in motion;
    May roll it faster than the fleeting wind,

Until Columbia is become as free
And independent as she ought to be.

And I admire those women, too, for daring
  To disregard the fooleries of the day:
To go to church and worship without caring
What of their dress Miss Shallowpate may
    say, —
Perhaps their bonnets may appear too flaring, —
  The fashion may be three months passed
    away, —
A plain and well-becoming dress they wear;
What fools may say they do not greatly care.

Right in this city I can find a score
  Of women, — widows and devoted mothers,
Who (though they are unfortunately poor)
  Would like to go to church as well as others.
But woman, she is woman the world o'er;
  Nor is she strong as are her stronger brothers, —
She cannot muster courage oft to go
And sit 'mid silks in dress of calico.

In Nature there is ever loveliness;
  Something pleasing always strikes the eye;
The useful bee appears in simple dress;
  Not so the brilliant, broad-winged butterfly;
The hen has clothing beautiful far less
  Than has the gaudy peacock strutting high;
And of mankind the same's the truth to-day:
Those of least use care most about display.

Behold our Franklin, true Republican!
    Look on him while he was ambassador
At Louis' court. The wealth of Hindostan
    His homespun he would not have left off for;
Because he was a patriotic man, —
    Did all the pomp of royalty abhor, —
Wise man and great! Baboons and apes the
      kind
That mimic, — never does the man of mind.

If I should e'er become a maniac,
    I hope it may be on account of love;
But ne'er a maid my brain I hope may crack,
    Unless it be Columbia, bright dove!
I 'd give her lips most willingly a smack;
    A fairer creature dwells there not above, —
'T is loving her too much, if now I 'm ailing, —
I 'm truly thankful if it is my failing.

How patriotic would the movement be
    To form ourselves into a mighty band,
A glorious " *Franklin Society,*"
    And drive the blight of Europe from our land;
Stand up in all our youthful strength, — be
      free!
    Kneel at the motion of no foreign wand, —
Let our ambition blaze like fiery Mars;
I 'd have the world enlightened by our stars!

Our ever-glorious stars! Already they
    Send forth a heavenly light upon the world;

They shine so brightly they are seen by day.
    Where is it that our banner when unfurled
Does not meet great respect?   Here dwells a
       fay —
A little fairy — (hair perhaps uncurled),
She visits sleeping men across the sea —
Gives hopeful dreams; her name is Liberty!

And we are free, we say; in " '76 "
    Our fathers fought and gained our liberty;
But all this freedom, I deem, goes for " *nichtz,*"
    If unto princes still we bow the knee;
If still to aliens we 're cemented bricks, —
    Glued on to France, or England, we 're not
       free!
Now every breeze that blows from cross the ocean
Causes a tip-up here, causes commotion.

In " '76," 't is said, our fathers armed
    Themselves against oppressive foreign king, —
Oppressive?   Yes, freemen felt greatly harmed
    At taxes placed on every little thing, —
On teas and so forth, and like bees they swarmed
    (A worn-out figure) and did sharply sting
The oppressor.   They drove him from the hive.
O Liberty, do heroes yet survive!

Of Fashion's great expense I 'll make slight men-
       tion;
    Let people spend their money as they please
The sanguinary, seven-long-years contention
    Our fathers had with George across the seas,

Rose from exactions of a less dimension
　　(And I have named the tax upon the teas)
Than what is levied by the tyrant Fashion —
By our wise rage to mimic the French nation.

Paris truly is a moral city;
　　So is Iago, too, an honest man;
Would we not worship " Paris " 't were a pity, —
　　Be our fair ladies all Parisian!
Modest, thoughtful, chaste, religious, witty
　　As well as handsome?　Mortal beings can
Array themselves in such a heavenly guise
You 'd deem they were descended from the skies!

'T is surely true; Olympus is deserted
　　By her she gods, and they are all come down —
Diana, Venus, Vesta, — all hooped-skirted
　　Walk gracefully the streets of western town, —
Europa, too; it can't be controverted;
　　For they are seen by city gent and clown.
Juno, Electra, Rhodea are seen
Oft promenading o'er the prairies green.

That they will notice cannot be expected
　　The poor, despised beings of this world, —
Widows, orphans hungry — almost naked, —
　　Down to perdition let the poor be hurled!
In blood they 're not with goddesses connected;
　　The same kind heavens o'er them are not
　　　　unfurled.
Of one blood, 't is true, all nations of the Earth
Were made; but goddesses had higher birth.

Oh, now it seems to me that I have read
   That One, divine, lived in an elder day,
Who " had not place whereon to lay His head."
   But " He was of a vulgar class," you say ;
" His place of birth was but an humble shed,
   And He slept in a manger on the hay."
He was *divine*, although so very meek
That no one lived to whom He would not speak.

But the Olympic female, she is great, —
   Nor does she care for those of low degree ;
She looks on Jesus Christ as " second rate," —
   A beautiful gilt Bible, though, has she ;
Indeed she is a Christian, sedate,
   And worships God quite fashionably ;
She says her dainty prayers like Pretty Polly, —
Worships *her* God, — kneels at the shrine of folly.

To follow Jesus Christ, the meek and lowly,
   " Sell all thou hast and give it to the poor ; " —
'T is with a vengeance done in this our holy
   Age and country. Go, lady, to the door ;
All that poor woman asks of thee is solely
   A crust of bread ; 't will not decrease thy store ;
Ah, give it ; take those jewels from thine ears —
Go sell them, Christian, dry the widow's tears !

The great Pythagoras no doubt had failed
   To lead the women of the days of old
To give up finery ; but he assailed
   Them with this clinching argument : " Behold,"

Said he, " I am a God!" — and so prevailed.
   They threw away e'en ornaments of gold.
His doctrines were, " That female loveliness
Consists in virtue ; not in showy dress."

If the Almighty in His Word should say
   " Let women adorn themselves in modest
Apparel, and not with costly array
      Of gold and pearls and 'broidered hair; 't were
         best
They meekness have, and do good works," — to-day
   Would Eve's fair daughters make of it a jest?
Would Honor, Beauty, Virtue not reply
" Thy will be done on Earth as 't is on High"?
      .   .   .   .

      June, 1860.

INTEMPERANCE.

FORBEAR, ambitious youth, thou canst not hope
To rival Dryden or immortal Pope;
Ah, venture not thy inexperienced pen
In measure sacred to these matchless men!
Thou canst not hope by these thy beardless lays
To twine about thy brow unfading bays;
Ah, never think by them to gain renown;
Forbear, or be the jest of all the town!

    To gain renown! 't is not for this I write;
Nor is 't my aim to vent malignant spite;
Howe'er, you may receive it as you please;
For I admit my liver 's not at ease —
A little grudge I have — it is n't much —
Against the Germans (vulgarly called Dutch).

    There was a time when Rome was unrefined;
She gained her polish from the Grecian mind;
From Athens all her early teachers came;
Inspired her sons with an ambitious flame;
'T was learned Greeks that raised her to that
      stage
To which she rose in her Augustine age.

    The God-like Germans come from cross the
      sea,
And so deserve our hospitality;

And therefore I shall treat them with respect;
I shall not comment on each nice defect;
They 're men of learning, as is known to all;
Their fame is spread o'er this terrestrial ball;
For seven long years each one was sent to
    school, —
Such is by law the universal rule, —
O learned men! how worthy of renown!
Thrice welcome here in each American town!
You bring refinement to our barbarous homes;
Transform our cities into glorious Romes!
    One mighty German now, behold I sing!
His store of learning was astonishing!
He knew the " Greek," the " Latin," and " He-
    brew ; "
" English," " Italian," and the " French," he
    knew, —
" Spanish " and " German," — on the banks of
    Rhine
Had knelt him long at Learning's sacred shrine.
Those tongues to him were merely household
    words ;
He might be truly classed 'mongst mocking-birds ;
He could repeat verbatim, the " Euclid ; "
Had all of " Aristotle " in his head ;
Had mastered all the learning of the " School ; "
He understood each old " Alchemic rule ; "
Familiar was with " Kepler " and " Laplace ; "
The constellations of the heavens could " trace ; "
To him all modern science, too, was known ;
Yet made but few discoveries of his own ;

He knew the lore of all of the sacred " Nine ; "
In short, he had exhausted Learning's mine, —
All that is found in books this man had read ;
And had it all housed safely in his head.
How he " refines " society now hear : —
He is a retailer of lager beer!
Is 't thus we see the German scholar seek
T" improve society just like a Greek ?

In early times there came a pious flock ;
Their children now oft kiss old Plymouth Rock ;
Immortal band ! Their history but read,
You 'll find that they were god-like men indeed —
A mighty empire to their God they found ;
To Him they consecrate each rood of ground ;
A thousand temples soon to Him arise ;
To Him they make a daily sacrifice ;
They wear a sober, ever-thoughtful face ;
They pray continually for Heavenly grace ;
Believe this maxim true : that no free state
Can be supported by the profligate.
Six days they labor busy in the field ;
The seventh unto their Maker's service yield ;
They honor Him this day the best they can ;
They spend it in a manner worthy man ;
Rest from their labors ; you can hear no noise ;
The matron keeps an eye upon her boys ;
Thousands remember thus the Sabbath day ;
Not one is found the " Book " to disobey ;
With temperance their frugal board is spread,
And God is thanked whenever they break bread ;

With seriousness their every act is fraught;
Their every deed is joined to earnest thought;
For they are men not led by foreign reins;
Yes, they are men that think with their own
　　　brains;
They hope that here may rise a Commonwealth,
That will live always in its native health.
　　　America, behold her then to-day!
All her magnificence can I portray!
The happy sequel of a golden dream!
How often has her glory been my theme!
A theme I love; how ready is my pen
To praise my country, and my countrymen!
I love her churches, Sabbaths, and free schools;
I hate the mimickers of foreign fools!
What soon may banish native virtue hence?
Naught but accursed foreign influence!
Must the wise lessons that our fathers taught
By us be disregarded — valued naught!
Their strict, pure manners must we now resign;
Receive new customs from the banks of Rhine?
Our Country's hope is in American youth, —
Oh, may they love religion, virtue, truth!
　　　Now for one moment let my pen move free;
I fain will picture what a boy should be —
What he *must* be, or not become a man;
Become, I mean, a true American;
Become a freeman worthy of the State
That has nor lord, nor prince, nor potentate.
First, then, his country he must dearly love,
Must love her truly like to God above;

Yes, patriotism; this must be a part
Of his religion — warm his youthful heart;
And he must learn a due respect to pay
To law; must learn to willingly obey
No tyrant, but let Justice have her sway;
And let him *think*, though he be out of school!
Close thinking 's seldom practised by a fool;
Such fools, for instance, as upon the street
We every day in mighty numbers meet,
Whose highest earthly aspirations are
To smoke most elegantly a cigar.

There 's not a meaner slave found in the South
Than he who has his master in his mouth;
He surely holds against himself a spite
Who lives enchained to " borrowed appetite."
I 'd rather now lie rotting in my grave,
Than be to that base hankering a slave!
My country's youth; I fain would have them be
High-minded, temperate, noble-hearted, free!
He that can rule himself, his soul, his mind,
Is greater than the conqueror of mankind;
First let me govern mine own self; and then
I shall be fit to govern other men.
Why is it that our country every year
Mourns thousands borne upon the drunkard's
            bier?
This to the vile tobacconist I tell:
'T is he that starts them on the road to hell!
They learn in early youth to sacrifice
To what should be contemned by all the wise;

They learn to chew tobacco and to smoke, —
Thus place their necks beneath the Devil's yoke!
Now he may drive them wheresoe'er he will!
You soon will see them visiting the Still.

Who are addicted to the pipe as much
As are the bloated-stomached German Dutch?
Ah, they puissant are in sleep, and staunch, —
It is the lager-beer that swells the p——h,
And makes them stupid like a snake that 's got
Within his bowels a huge ox to rot!
A foaming gallon in them ever raves;
It froths and bubbles, surges like sea-waves;
The storms that in their stomachs sometimes rise,
Behold the waves rise to the vaulted skies!
The Trojan fleet is scattered on the main;
Will Æneas e'er see his ships again?
The Dutch are not as sleepy as they seem —
Are not asleep when they appear to dream.
Of th' outward world they seldom heed the din;
Their eyes are turned to view the storms within.
"The Isles of Greece!" — while seated on a rock,
The "modern Greek" beholds the surge's shock,
Surveys the broad and sublime Ægean —
The "German Ocean" 's in the inner-man —
The German views it — sees its rising storms
And his big heart with patriotism warms.
"Hand down," says he, "quick, quick, my shield
       and spear!
I must defend the cause of lager beer!
Did I not leave my much-loved ' Fader-land '

And cross the ocean to this western strand,
Because 't was called a land of liberty?
Shall it the privilege withhold from me
Of drinking beer? This right I will maintain
Or cleave the vile oppressor through the brain!
At least I will not vote for men who fear
To legislate in favor of our beer!"

Thus speaks the Dutchman; and his speech ap-
    palls
Those who hold seats in legislative halls;
Their lips turn pale; their knees begin to quake;
In every joint and member see them shake!
Thus the wroth Dutchman's direful threats they
    fear,
And soon the laws are changed to favor beer.
And thus our wise Lycurguses gain votes!
See them in doggeries moistening their throats!
Gamblers, rum-sellers, ... and bloats
They court. The people's money waste. Their
    time
They spend winking at drunkenness and crime;
They make mock laws, pretending to put down
Intemperance. But still in every town
You 'll find a score of grog-shops. Why? Be-
    cause
They form the statute without any clause
To give 't effect. Better empower some one
To go about the streets with rope and gun,
And shoot or hang each whelp within his den
That with his poisonous fangs is biting men, —

Each villain that holds out to man the bowl,
To blast the joys of life and damn the soul.

There lives within my heart the deepest hate
Toward those reptiles, licensed by the State
To vend their poison. If I had the power
I 'd hang each cursed scoundrel ere an hour!
Why should they live? The poisonous rattlesnake
Seems harmless when of these a view we take ; —
Behold the woe and wretchedness they make!
Ah, mothers mourn, and children cry for bread ;
And hope is lost, and happiness is fled!
O Legislators, listless do ye stand
While Vice and Drunkenness run riot o'er the
         land!

Behold those boys upon the Sabbath day!
To th' house of God do they go up and pray?
No, they are boys 'scaped from the Sabbath-school
To see the German skeptics act the fool.
At the Dutch brewery upon the hill
The Germans spend their Sabbaths drinking swill,
And with their women waltz the livelong day,
While their brass bands sonoriously play,
Disturbing those who, on their native sod,
Would, like their fathers, love to worship God.
How superstitious! Do not know the truth!
Are not enlightened like the Dutch, forsooth!
Now a staunch German gets upon a box,
And thus he preaches doctrines orthodox : —
" Come, boys, in wassail learn to spend your days ;

Despise Religion ; it the brain will craze ;
Dance, smoke tobacco, drink, have cheer ;
Who would for sake of Heaven forego good beer ?
Drink and be merry on until you die ;
A future world is only in the eye !
Go, take your guns, and hunt on Sundays ; go !
" The laws " — ought any one regard them ?   No !
The Sunday laws ! Of Puritanic fools
Your cringing Representatives are tools !
Those stringent laws must soon be done away ;
Let Sunday be as any other day !
'T is but a Jewish relic at the best, —
Are not the Jews of all the world the jest ?
The Legislature has no right to make
Such laws, from men their liberties to take ! "

'T is thus the bloated, beer-drunk skeptics preach
And by their words and ill-bred actions teach.
A nobler band of freemen never trod
The Earth, than gave this Commonwealth to
        God —
Or, rather, they received the gift from Him.
My countrymen, this is no idle whim, —
Regard this truth : *The Bible is the rock
On which our government is built, and braves each
        threatening shock.*

August, 1860.

7

POESY.

A LYRIC.

ADDRESSED TO MY ESTEEMED FRIEND, REV. J. A. NASH.

POESY.

———

PART FIRST.

WHY it is I strike the string
　　Why it is I touch the lyre;
　Why like Orpheus would sing;
Why would wake Promethean fire?

Let me tell in pleasing words,
　Mingled with a lovely sound,
Like the singing of sweet birds
　That the huntsman dare not wound, —

Dare not kill the turtle dove,
　Dare not kill the little wren
Singing in the leafy grove,
　Gladdening the homes of men.

Are not sweet the words of praise
　That to virtue poets give?
It is in immortal lays
　That the just may ever live, —

Ever live upon the earth,
　Though their bodies be in dust, —

Thus will never perish worth;
   Thus shall never die the just.

Oh that I a song could frame,
   Lasting as the granite stone!
Then would never die his name;
   Ever would his fame be known,

Who has been my loving friend;
   Who has been my friend in need;
Never till my days shall end
   Can I pay him half his meed.

Could I live a thousand years,
   Blest with strength of mind and limb,
All this time too short appears
   To obtain reward for him.

Nash first lifted up my hands,
   First aroused my dormant mind
Pointed where Fame's temple stands;
   He gave vision to the blind.

God-like man, the thanks receive
   Of a truly grateful heart;
But I now sincerely grieve
   That I have not perfect art,

Cannot build the pleasing rhyme
   That eternal praise might give;

If your name must die in Time,
  In Eternity 't will live!

Thus it is the voice of song
  Rises in the good man's praise;
Thus it would his fame prolong,
  That men may in future days

Emulate his worthy deeds
  And arise to his repute;
Thus the poet sows good seeds
  That may ripen into fruit.

PART SECOND.

DEIGN to listen while I tell
How the poet's useful song
Fearless battles conduct fell; —
It opposes every wrong.

Like Clorinda, warrior maid,
Raging on the bloody field,
Wielding her puissant blade,
Causes every foe to yield.

Those that yield not to her arms —
Yield not to her sword or spear —
She can conquer by her charms —
Hear of fair Armida, hear!

Ten bold knights she captive took;
Led them o'er a distant sea;
Conquered them by her sweet look, —
'T was Rinaldo set them free.

But he yielded to her power!
He was vanquished by her might, —
Charméd in her pleasant bower,
How escaped the valiant knight?

To th' enchanted island came,
Guided by a wizard old,

Two brave champions of fame, —
   They released the warrior bold.

But she followed through the air, —
   Met him on the battle-field ;
Bravely fought this princess fair, —
   Naught then saved him but his shield.

Oh the powerful darts she cast
   While in radiant arms she shone !
Rinald' honored her at last, —
   Placed the princess on her throne.

Ever honored be the bard ;
   What is grief the poet learns ;
Tasso's lot in life was hard ;
   So was that of patriot Burns.

But how little does he care
   Where he rests his aching head,
Or how humble be his fare, —
   Only that he may have bread.

Never covetous his mind ;
   Free from every base desire ;
He, to benefit mankind,
   Lives, — what purpose can be higher ?

Is it not the poet gives
   Highest praise to God above ?

Every creature, too, that lives
  Has the poet's heartfelt love.

Now the falchion is bright, —
  It had rusted 'gainst the wall, —
See, he hastens to the fight,
  Willing, at his country's call.

Armed and doubly armed is he!
  Will the morning star grow dim?
Shudders dreadful Tyranny!
  Hears the glorious Marseilles Hymn!

Fearful as ten thousand swords
  Flashing in the sun's bright rays,
Are the poet's flaming words,
  When 'gainst Tyranny they blaze.

PART THIRD.

LISTEN longer if you can;
   I your kindness may requite;
Does not poesy to man
   Give angelical delight?

This is not hyperbole;
   Listen still to what I tell;
If you would your likeness see,
   Go and look into a well.

There you may behold your face
   Pictured truthfully, each part —
Its uncomeliness and grace —
   But the likeness of the heart!

Look in Shakspeare's silvery spring,
   By sweet Avon in the shade;
There the human heart — each string —
   Each pulsation is displayed.

Oh waters of that fount!
   Sweet as Juliet's blushing lips!
On Olympus' lofty mount
   Jove less pleasant nectar sips!

Enter into Paradise!
   Seek elysian groves of bliss!

Drink sweet waters without price!
  Live with lovely Beatrice!

The true poet has delights
  Quite unknown to other men;
Talks with angels, fairies, sprites,
  In the shady grove and glen.

Rock, and shell, and herb, and tree,
  He beholds with interest fraught;
Swallow, grasshopper, or bee
  Leads him into pleasant thought.

Wise Anacreon, thy name
  Fades not in the mist of years!
Thy sweet songs, so worthy fame,
  How delightful to my ears!

Were she banished from this sphere —
  The fair damsel Poesy!
Never to on earth appear,
  This were not the world for me!

Starry skies to love no more?
  Love no more the evening cloud?
Or my native lake's sweet shore? —
  I would seek the burial shroud!

To forego for shining gold
  Milton, Shakspeare, Collins, Burns!
These my anxious arms infold;
  While my soul the lucre spurns!

I would consecrate my life
  To the service of mankind:
Enter on a noble strife,
  Worthy of the loftiest mind.

And my humble efforts may
  Lead some youth to take the lyre;
One whose mind — the orb of day!
  One whose heart — a world of fire!

He will make mankind rejoice
  That he lived upon the Earth;
Praise with universal voice
  The proud land that gave him birth.

June, 1860.

MISCELLANEOUS POEMS.

THE POET.

S mighty as the sun's meridian flame,
　　Among the nations glows the poet's
　　mind,
Enlightening and blessing all mankind.
How few have lived to merit his proud name!
Thy harp, O David, vibrates still on earth,
　　Hymning melodiously Jehovah's praise;
　　Isaiah, thou thy voice in song didst raise;
And Jeremiah, thine the poet's birth.
How high the honored calling of the Bard!
　　His God-given trust, how sacred and sublime!
Religion, Truth, and Virtue's watchful guard, —
　　A sentinel upon the tower of time, —
Yes, Uriel in shining armor dressed,
Immortal honor beaming from his crest.

July 4th, 1867.

8

TO MY BOY.

My darling boy, ere yet thou canst repeat
Thy father's name; and when thy little feet
Can just bear up thy frame; and thou dost sit
Upon her knee who bore thee, and dost fold
Thine arms about her neck, and fondly kiss
The cheek suffused with tears, — thy mother's
    cheek, —
What is it, child, that saddens so her heart?
These tears are shed for thee. She asks of Him,
The mighty Father, in His love, a boon, —
But first, she thanks Him for the joy He gave
In granting her this blessed little babe, —
Her light, her hope, her happiness of soul!
My son, thy mother's heart dost ask that thou
May'st " grow in favor both with God and
    man ";
Not always wilt thou be as thou art now,
Protected by a mother's watchful care;
But soon thou must arise to man's estate
And meet the stern realities of life.
Thy mother asks that God may take thy hand
And lead thee safely in life's rugged path,
Lest Satan tempt thee from the happy way,
And in the wilderness leave thee to starve.
How dreary is the wilderness of sin!

Behold the drunkard wandering without hope!
Behold him fall into the deep abyss!
He sinks beneath the waves of dark Despair!
Blessed is he who ruleth his own soul!
His passions lead him not where'er they will;
This man is free; he feareth only God;
Before His Throne of Grace, he oft doth bow,
And stretcheth forth his hands in humble prayer.
It is his privilege to worship Him;
And true philosophy of mind doth place
The faculty of prayer as King indeed
Above the others. When it reigns supreme
It giveth motion to the good in man;
He that loves God will love God's creatures.
How great a joy the Christian heart doth feel,
In prayerful meditation before God;
The upper window of the soul thrown ope,
A flood of light flows in and gladdens all.
It is thy parents' hope, my son, that thou
Wilt lead a Christian life — wilt ofttimes pray
To Him who far above the clouds doth sit
Upon His throne of might, — a King, indeed,
But still a Father kind, whose gentle love
Doth bless each living thing. " A sparrow falls
Not to the ground without His care." My child,
Like God, do right, because 't is right; do thou
Love God, because He first loved thee; and let
Thy highest pleasure be, to contemplate
His wondrous works; to study deep His laws,
Adoring Him the while. The Bible take
In thy right hand and press it to thy heart, —

The richest gift of God to man. Wisdom,
My boy, of Hume, nor Gibbon, nor Voltaire,
Could shake the " Sacred Truth."   It still survives
The Book of Books, the Holy Book of God!
These are no hollow sounding words, my child ;
And he, who tries to walk without this Light,
Will grope his way in darkness evermore.
The heart of man, without a steadfast hope,
Without reliance on the Word of God,
With doubts arising ever in the mind,
Is desolate beyond what tongue can tell.

December, 1864.

MOTHER.

O MOTHER, could I but uprear to thee
    A monument immortal as thy love!
    Thou dwellest, mother, in the courts above,
From ills of life, from sorrow ever free.
Thou hadst not, mother, aught of vanity;
    But thou, a Christian woman, ever strove
    In holy walks and in the heavenly grove
To lead thy children ever lovingly;
Nor books perused, except the Book of God.
    To thee, in childhood, learning was denied;
But ever in the path of duty trod
    With holy zeal, and Jesus was thy guide;
Religion was a crown about thy brow;
Mother, *I know* thou art an angel now.

July, 1865.

ANDREW T. BLODGETT.

HEROIC boy, is this thy grave?
  It is new made. This oaken board —
Is 't fit memorial to the brave
  Who for his country drew his sword?

Thou hast a fairer monument;
  'T is Freedom's ensign, with its stars;
Ah, blood redeemed that flag, unrent,
  Untarnished, from the hand of Mars.

And freely, warmly flowed thine own;
  Because thou wast a patriot true,
Thy country's glory on thee shone;
  Thy country's greatness passed in view.

And now, methinks, I hear thee tell
  What rapture in thy bosom rose
When thou didst scorn both Death and Hell,
  Defiant of thy country's foes!

I kneel and kiss thy grave; my tears,
  So warm, bedew the crumbling clod;
I consecrate anew my years
  To country, liberty, and God!

Now peacefully with Jasper rest,
  And Lawrence — hero of the sea !
Ah, thou hast joined the patriots blest
  Who fought at old Thermopylæ.

May 5th, 1866.

M. M. CROCKER.

How bright a record this brave man has made!
  The hero stood midst shot and bursting shell
  Unharmed. Where "Death reigned King" and
    thousands fell,
On high he wielded his victorious blade.
But now aside he has the sabre laid,
  And gone, in everlasting peace to dwell.
  Had he not lived and fought, ah! who can tell
If e'en to-day would War's red tide be stayed!
His prowess won the field at Champion Hill,
  And ope'd the way for Vicksburg to be ta'en;
And it was his indomitable will
  That gained the day at Jackson. For the slain
He wept. Our country 's saved, and peace is
    won ;
Brave Crocker has gone home; his work is done.

August 29th, 1865.

ABIGAIL FREDERICK.

When Corwin died, thy hope, thy darling boy,
  A victim of the Southern, *Davis* hate —
  Perished a martyr to preserve the State —
With him departed, Abigail, thy joy.
'T is true he died a soldier's death; but then
  Rebellion slew the mother with the son;
  Her flesh and blood he was, — their hearts were
    one.
Thy wrath, O God, be hot 'gainst wicked men!
Thou wast a Christian, truly, Abigail;
  With heart most kind, — of Christ-like tender-
    ness,
  Nor wanting fortitude in deep distress, —
But love too strong bore thee beyond the vale.
Thou 'st met thy boy where sorrow is unknown;
Art seated with him on a shining throne.

  May 24th, 1867.

N. W. MILLS.

WHAT nobler man has fallen in the war!
  Of talents rare; to poesy inclined;
  Young, brave, religious, polished, ever kind;
A pioneer in Art, — was known afar, —
The West can illy spare his rising star;
  A patriot true, he perished in his prime;
  His name will live with Warren's through all
      time;
Nor will a blot his page in hist'ry mar.
Ah, death must come! If on the field of fame.
  When battling for our native land, we die,
We leave behind an ever-glorious name,
  That will be blest while ages shall pass by.
Now peaceful is the land for which he fought;
But with his blood our peace was dearly bought.

  Dec. 1864.

WILLIAM P. BRANNAN.

Brannan is dead! Commendable regard
  Thou showest, Ohio, for thy poet son;
  Abundant flowers upon his grave thou 'st
      strewn.
When sung there e'er a truer, sweeter Bard?
His gems of song shine like the sun in heaven,
  And brightly will they glow through passing
      years,
  Melting true hearts to tenderness and tears, —
Upon the earth no gentler soul has striven.
The "painter-poet" labored not for wealth,
  But to increase the glory of his land;
Dread disappointments broke his tender health,
  And cruel poverty's relentless hand.
Now "storms of fate pursue his steps no more,
And rainbows bloom where all was black before."

May, 1867.

ADALINE.

She was so tender, loving, meek and mild!
　　Ah, parents, sisters, brothers, now repine;
　　For Death hath taken little Adaline!
Her grave is in the lonely forest wild;
And she 's among the pure and undefiled,
　　Where none will ever her bright fame malign.
　　Why I am sad I cannot well define;
In Heaven far happier is the blessed child!
To lose a loving sister or a brother,
　　Although we know they have gone home to
　　　God,
Or see departing a beloved mother,
　　Hear rattling on her coffin-lids the clod —
It wrings the heart; it rends the soul amain.
Ah, never more will come bright joy again!

July, 1865.

On yonder hill stood Keokuk, not many years
    ago,
And cast a sorrowing glance upon the beauteous
    plain below.
The Autumn sun was setting then; the moon
    was in her wane;
And sorrow filled the Indian's heart; his bosom
    heaved with pain;
For where these noble rivers twain their crystal
    waters join,
Then flaunted proudly to the breeze the flag o'er
    Fort Des Moines.
He thought how Keokuk had been ever the white
    man's friend,
Had helped to bring the hopeless war of Black
    Hawk to an end;
And now the mandate had gone forth, — "The
    Indian must away;
Nor in this land another moon could he prolong
    his stay."
He gazed upon the joyless sky; he gazed upon
    the stream;
At last his soul burst forth in words; he talked
    as in a dream:
"Enough, enough, the white man hath two
    tongues; though pale his cheek,

His heart is black, and, like the wolf, he preys
    upon the weak.
The Sac and Fox were once proud names, a
    terror in the land ;
Ah, now no longer men and braves, but women
    I command.
Black Hawk stood up and faced the foe; I called
    it useless strife ;
I sought to check the tide of blood ; but now I
    hate my life !
I gave bad counsel to my friends ; Black Hawk
    my words betrayed ;
Oh, had I now his stalwart braves I'd vindicate
    his shade !
It is too late ; with drink unnerved, the Indian
    is a slave ;
The *fire-water* hath burnt up the valor of the
    brave.
The wolf Remorse now eats my heart; I, like a
    woman, weep ;
Oh that my grave were made, that I might with
    my fathers sleep ! "

    .   .   .   .   .   .

There is no marble slab to mark the humble
    spot of earth,
'Neath which reposes Keokuk, the man of match-
    less worth.
'Bove him the plowshare turns the sod, and corn
    grows on his grave ;
But his renown can never die, while live the
    good and brave.

Nov. 1865.

MY NATIVE VILLAGE.

TO ROLLIN E. DEFREES.

My native village by the lake,
Gladly a pilgrimage I 'd make, —
Revisit thee, and paddle o'er
The lovely lake from shore to shore!
I 'd stand again on " Indian Hill," —
Is it as wild and lonely still
As it was when, a gleeful boy,
I clambered over it with joy?
Dear Rollin, have you now forgot
Those happy moments? I have not.
'T was yesterday that we forsook
The school-room for the babbling brook;
'T was yesterday our fluttermills
Were whirling in the rapid rills;
Ah, naught could then disturb our joys;
We knew no grief; for we were boys.
On " Cedar Point " do cedars grow
As they did twenty years ago?
And is the " Big Lake," too, as wild
As when I played, a happy child?
Those islands, too, do they appear
The same, and are they filled with deer?
" All these are changed," I hear you say;
" The forests old are swept away;

The lonely islands now are bare;
The rabbit only shelters there."

My native village by the lake,
Unhappy memories awake;
How sad the pictures of the past!
The sky with woe is overcast.
I see a widow, wan and old,
Whose sorrows never can be told.
Ah, once the child of hope and wealth,
And love, and gayety, and health;
Sweet days, at first, like falling snow;
At last, an avalanche of woe!
Husband and wife and children blest,
They came so hopeful to the West;
A wilderness before them lay;
A garden it shall bloom one day.
  "The lovely lake in beauty smiles,
    The lovely lake with all its isles;
    It shall obey me with its force;
    My wealth is in this watercourse."
The might of man was here displayed;
He spake the word; the waves obeyed.
In wrath, and to avenge the wrong,
(So I will have it in my song,)
The guardian naiads of the lake,
A sure and speedy vengeance take:
  "Arise, ye waves, and sweep away
  Man's puny works!"
             The waves obey.
He who was rich, to-day is poor,

And Want stands frowning at his door.
"And you, ye mists, with poisonous breath,
    Go, bear abroad destroying death!"
The many grassy mounds attest
How was obeyed the grim behest; —
Behold, the strong man bows his head,
And Rachel mourns her children dead.

My native village by the lake,
A sorrowful pilgrimage I 'll make
When I revisit thee again, —
My feeling heart will throb with pain;
For there, alas, her grave was made;
She sleeps beneath the oak tree's shade.
Her monument is in my heart;
That mother's teachings are my chart,
My guide of life; she prayed; she wept;
Until the sleep of death she slept!
What, needs the Christian mother, say,
A marble slab above her clay?
Her monument will ne'er decay!
It is immortal as the soul
Of him who felt her sweet control.
The Christian mother's prayers and tears
Are not forgot through circling years.

Dec. 1865.

WEALTH AND HAPPINESS.

TO B. F. ALLEN.

HE is a jealous God that rules above.
To-day, like Crœsus, we rejoice in wealth;
To-morrow, poor, we groan like him in chains.
When Sherman swept, with his avenging host,
Through Georgia and the Carolinas, then
What desolation marked his path! The wealth
Of thousands, and their homes, in smoke
Ascended to the clouds. Cities were burned,
And many that were proud, whose homes had
    been
Palaces, took shelter in low hovels,
And now are poor, and labor for their bread.
   True happiness dwells wholly in the mind —
Is seated in the heart — a gift of God; —
Resting on virtue, 't is securely fixed.
The youth accustomed to a home of comfort, —
A bed to sleep on, like a downy pillow,
Goes forth to battle in his country's service.
The earth is now his bed; the sky his shelter.
Long days he marches — joins in dreadful con-
    flicts —
Is he unhappy? No. About the camp-fire,
Late in the evening, when the dead lie buried,

He and his comrades cheerily are talking.
The rebel has been driven, and the soldier
Was never happier at his father's fire-side.
Man has his joys in every situation.

What profit is it, then, to build fine dwellings,
And till the soil and cultivate the vine,
If man, when living in the mountain caverns,
Chasing wild beasts and eating roots and gar-
    bage,
Was just as happy as he is to-day?
He reaches forth and grasps at the ideal;
Not satisfied with his condition now,
Anticipates a better, happier future.
He sees the golden apples in the distance,
But when he plucks them, lo! they turn to
    ashes.
A cabin, where there's plenty and contentment,
Is as desirable as is the palace.
God has assigned us all a work to do: —
To make the world the better and the wiser
And the happier for our living in it.
He that has wealth should use it. Let him build
A dwelling of surpassing beauty. Walks
And arbors, trees and gushing fountains,
Let them appear in beauty all around it.
Thus he affords the laboring man employment,
And all the beauties of his home are common.
The poor, delighted, look upon his gardens;
Fragrance is borne upon the breeze, and gladdens
All who come near the bounteous habitation.
The growing West has yielded him possessions;

For honestly and nobly has he labored.
His name engraven, as in polished marble,
Upon the bulwark of the public welfare,
Will bright appear throughout recurring ages.

May, 1867.

"COMMON MEN."

We live, indeed, in an historic age;
Bright names illuminate the shining page;
The name of Grant, four years ago, who knew?
Old Time can ne'er efface that name from view;
And Lincoln — in how short a time has fame
Recorded high his ever-glorious name!
Yes, in remotest climes is Lincoln known;
His praise to-day is heard in every zone.
And he deserves the fame the world bestows;
To him our country her salvation owes.
Lincoln and Grant — in these few words I tell
Their whole career — *they did their duties well.*

Does not the faithful soldier in the "ranks"
As well deserve a grateful people's thanks?
Had Abraham Lincoln died unknown and poor,
Within his father's humble cabin door,
From wounds received in battling savage men,
He would have died at post of duty then,
And in the sight of God appeared as great,
As when he died the saviour of the State.

How many noble men are lost to fame!
How many heroes die without a name!

Had Charles but kept the people's good in view,
Then Cromwell 'd have continued ale to brew;
And had the South concluded to obey,
Grant would, no doubt, be bartering *hides* to-day.
So, every day, in busy walks we meet,
In mart, in work-shop, on the crowded street,
Men, who in life an humble part perform,
But who, if called to battle with the storm,
Would meet it boldly, as did old King Lear, —
Their arms are strong; their hearts unknown to
    fear ;
They know their worth ; their modesty 's as
    great ;
They are the nation's strength — *they are the*
    State !
A nation's fame is theirs; their voice, their nod,
The great world heeds — the fiat of a god!

May, 1865.

"RIGHTS."

Upon our nation's natal day
  The tear-drop glistens in my eye,
To see with glorious display
  Our banner floating in the sky.

I love the flag. The soldier, too,
  In battle loves his trusty gun,
Because it is his guardian true, —
  The flag protects each patriot son.

If in a foreign land I roam, —
  E'en on Morocco's burning sands;
Far, far from kindred and from home, —
  It saves me from the tyrant's hands.

Has it not, too, the power to save
  From tyranny *at home* as well?
Yes, it proclaimed, " Be free, O slave!"
  A thunderbolt from Heaven fell

And broke all manacles and chains.
  Our flag proclaims " Equality."
The ancient God of Israel reigns;
  Americans everywhere are free!

What of " State Rights ? " The good old flag—
  (The millions move) 't is in the van;
Inscribed upon the glorious rag
  Is " God,". and " Equal rights of man ! "

" State Rights ! " — it is a cheat, a lie!
  If each *man* has his rights, 't is well;
For *individual* rights I cry,
  And State Rights may remain in Hell!

July 4th, 1866.

TO " CRITICS."

I am unawed by all that fools may say;
  Clearly in Faith's stereoscope I see
  My own America, the great and free,
In her munificence proudly repay
With wreath of fame, the Bard whose patriot lay
  Defends, in name of God, sweet Liberty.
  It matters not how wise the " Critics " be;
It matters not how lion-like they bray;
With hope undaunted, still unmoved I stand.
  Thou art, my country, worthy of my love;
I look with pride upon my native land,
  And bow my knee to none but God above.
My harp is rough — a chip from Plymouth Rock;
Its strings — the fibre of the " Charter Oak."

  May, 1866.

SONNET.

ON SEEING GENERAL SHERMAN IN DES MOINES, OCTOBER 7TH, 1865.

I LOVE my country, and the chief who led
   Our brothers — gallant men — to victory.
   He is the embodiment of energy;
Unfading wreaths of laurel crown his head —
And he deserves bright bays, whose deeds have
     shed
   Such lustre on our land of liberty —
   Have given her the proudest history:
During all time 't will be with wonder read —
   The daring march through Georgia to the coast
And on o'er proud Carolina's dismal wold;
   Magnanimous toward the conquered host,
He is beloved for manly heart and bold;
And though "detractions rude" assail his name,
They cannot dim his star of well-earned fame.

TO MY BROTHER.

When War's dread clarion rang in " '61,"
  And Crocker called our brave young men to
    arms,
  You rushed, dear brother, into War's alarms,
And bore most soldierly your trusty gun!
Brave Weeks and Doty fell at Donelson;
  Loved comrades sleep on Shiloh's bloody plain;
  At Corinth many fell 'midst leaden rain; —
Ah, see dark clouds arise; fierce work is done,
  Where bold McPherson renders up his life!
  And you were, brother, near him in the strife;
Beheld the flames devour Atlanta's pride;
  And, at Savannah, saw the boundless sea;
Stood by the flag until Rebellion died;
  Are coming home, — with joy we welcome
    thee!

July, 1865.

THE PARTING.

THE war is over now, my boys;
    Our country is restored;
Unbuckle now your harness, boys;
    Lay by the gun and sword.

Oh, how we love the flag, my boys!
    It was the winding-sheet
Of many of our comrades, boys,
    Whose hearts have ceased to beat.

We are a band of brothers, boys;
    Our love 's increased with years;
Though we 're unused to weep, my boys,
    We part with many tears!

We 've planted high our banner, boys;
    On high it must remain;
If foreign foes assail it, boys,
    We 'll shoulder arms again.

August, 1865.

THE ORPHAN'S SONG.

PAPA listed in the army,
   And left mamma, Jane, and I
Weeping in our lonely cottage, —
   Little baby said, " By, by."

By, by, papa, — gone forever!
   Now he lies beneath the sod ;
He was murdered by a traitor,
   But his spirit is with God.

Loving friends have given money
   And endowed a pleasant home —
Home and school for orphan children, —
   See the children hither come !

Come and join in happy chorus,
   Praise the land we love so well ;
May our banner float forever
   O'er the field where papa fell !

June, 1865.

LINES.

God is our only King;
Let us in gladness sing, —
Shout on the land and sea
Union and Liberty!

We will deal justly, then,
As becomes noble men;
Shout on the land and sea
Union and Charity.

God is our only King;
Let us His praises sing, —
Shout on the land and sea
Union and Victory!

March, 1866.

PEACE.

Praise God, the mighty King of kings,
  That now, at His command,
Sweet Peace has spread her golden wings
  Above our weeping land!

To help the rich the war began;
  It ended for the poor;
And taught the world, " The common man
  Is King for evermore."

The maxim of mankind has been
  " The many for the few ; "
See Freedom's era now begin,
  And lordlings sink from view!

April, 1866.

THE FLAG.

DECEMBER, 1862.

Columbia's flag, — hope of the world! —
  Its folds shall ne'er be torn ;
Triumphant through this bloody war
  I see it onward borne!

The willing arm that lifts on high
  The ensign of the free, —
That spreads the starry banner forth,
  On land and on the sea, —
The youthful arm, the patriot arm,
  It palsied must not be!

Strike down the craven wretch who cries,
  " Our ensign, let it fall ;
And on the sea no more be seen,
  And on the fortress wall ! "

A half a million heroes now
  Are on the tented field,
And up to God has gone their vow
  To die before they 'll yield.

A half a million more will leave
  Sweet babes and loving wives,

And for the Union and the flag
  Will freely give their lives.

Think not, you base-born coward, e'er
  The brave will ask to stay
The gushing tide of blood and death
  Before the foe gives way ;

Before upon old Sumter's walls
  Our banner is unfurled;
Before the Union is confessed
  As *one* by all the world.

.   .   .   .   .   .

Then howl no more, ye craven crew,
  For dastard compromise,
Lest earth soon cover you from view,
  And death bedim your eyes !

10

AN ADDRESS

TO THE SOLDIERS' ORPHANS.

RESPECTFULLY INSCRIBED TO REV. PEARL P. INGALLS, FOUNDER OF
THE IOWA ORPHANS' HOME.

Your fathers loved the banner well;
Beneath its hallowed folds they fell.

Their blood redeemed the land we love;
Their spirits rest with God above.

None ever found a prouder grave
Than those who died our homes to save.

They happ'ly lived and nobly died;
Their mem'ry is the nation's pride;

And ye, blest children, stand to-day
The nation's mightiest strength and stay!

For tenderest recollections, twined
About your hearts, endear and bind

That flag to you. Unending woe
To him who is our country's foe!

But other foes ye must withstand,
Than those who wield the sword and brand;

E'en now they 're holding dire debate
How they may overturn the State.

Behold their hosts are marshalled, — lo!
They overwhelm the land with woe!

Prepare, then, speed'ly for the fight;
Gird on your glowing armor bright!

Ah, Knowledge is an ample shield;
Grasp it, and hasten to the field!

And Virtue is a trenchant sword;
But seize the mightiest spear, — God's Word!

Go forth, as David did of old,
And lay the dreadful giant cold.

Behold Intemperance stalking forth, —
Ah, let the demon bite the earth!

Our nation never had, I know,
In darkest hour, a deadlier foe.

Who loves his country now, arise
And smite the monster till it dies!

There never has such cause been given,
Why men should pattern after Heaven,

As God has from His bounteous hand
Bestowed on those of our loved land.

The proudest birthright ever known
Do we this moment call our own.

What blood and wretchedness and pain
Has 't cost this happy boon to gain!

'T is only Virtue that can save
It from Destruction's whelming wave.

Ah, then what argument that you
(Whose parents' blood was shed like dew,

To gain the liberties we prize,
And save our ensign of the skies) —

What argument that you should aim
To win, on earth, a God-like name!

Ah, keep your hands from every sin
And brightest wreaths of Learning win!

Knowledge and Virtue are a wall
Invulnerable 'gainst cannon ball.

The State, when fenced by these around,
Defies all enemies 'bove ground.

Oh what a blessed land have we!
It is the freest of the free!

God bless immortal Lincoln's name;
'T is written on the scroll of fame;

With Washington's 't is blazing high —
Two mighty suns risen in mid sky —

With equal brilliancy they glow,
And beautify the world below!

How proud I am that I can claim
The honor of the American name!

Was born upon the happy soil,
That blesses thus a son of toil;

For noblest men oft wield the sledge,
Or guide the plow, or drive the wedge.

Here Honor's doors wide open swing
To give them seats above a king.

No castes are here, and *all* are free; —
God bless our land of liberty!

October 5th, 1865.

HAPPINESS.

THERE is a soul-land. Lost from all things real,
  The spirit wanders amid bowers of pleasure;
  Bright angels sparkle brilliant beyond meas-
    ure —
All 's light and love in this fair land ideal.
Where is this soul-land? Every human being
  Has it within, — ah, beautiful, supernal!
  It is in miniature the Heaven Eternal;
'T is Eden, planted by the Great All-Seeing.
But who may wander in the lovely Aidenn?
  The gates are open of the fields Elysian,
  And I can see no mortal in my vision,
But may pass in and be with pleasures laden.
  Ah, enter in, and live with love forever, —
  From Virtue, Hope, Content, be parted never

July, 1865.

TO MY SISTER.

And thou art far away, my sister dear;
    The Rocky Mountains look down on thy
      home;
    They rise above and pierce the heavenly
      dome;
The roaring of their torrents smites thy ear;
The piercing winds that through the canyons
      sweep,
    Chill thee in Winter with their biting cold;
The snow-capped summits of the rocky steep,
    Display a beauty I would glad behold.
Thou rockest thy belovéd boy to sleep,
    Remembering brothers, sisters, father old,
Far, far away, — and thou dost, sister, weep,
    But soon art comforted; thy husband bold,
Though savages may threaten dread alarms,
Enwraps thee safely in his loyal arms.

July, 1865.

TO MY WIFE.

Say, darling, dost thou deem that now I love thee,
  As when we wandered in the bright ideal,
  Ere we were one in union Hymeneal?
Far brighter, dearest, shines my star above thee!
Oft thou in tender kindness dost reprove me,
  For being so enwrapped in the unreal —
  And sorrowest, too; because thou canst not
      see all
The hidden motives that so strangely move me.
I sit alone with pen in hand and write,
  Seeming indifferent toward my loving wife,
  And little children, — darlings of my life!
So lost upon Parnassus' rugged height.
  Oh think not, dearest, that my love's declining;
  It is the sun, far up in heaven shining.

July, 1865.

POESY.

Is Poesy, then, only garden flowers,
    That, cultivated with a kindly care,
    With beauty glow, and sweetly scent the air,
And lovers languish in the leafy bowers?
'T is might, — behold the dreaded lion cowers
    (Before the strong man) smitten in his lair;
    See the fierce Norman slay the Russian bear!
'T is beauty not unlike the smiling Hours!
'T is might and beauty gracefully combined.
    See Dian in the groves with bow and quiver;
She slays the tusky boar, pursues the hind;
    She views her radiant tresses in the river;
And, chaste in beauty, blesses all mankind.
    Ah, God to man of Poesy 's the giver!

July, 1865.

HOPE.

So brilliantly it shines to-night,
  The glorious star of even;
Thus in my soul is beaming bright
  My hope of Earth and Heaven.

My toils, my prayers are not in vain,
  (For God and right I 've striven,)
On Earth bright honor I shall gain;
  A golden crown in Heaven.

EARLIER POEMS.

—◆—

TO A CHILD.

LITTLE Mary, come to me;
   Come and sit upon my knee;
   Happy cherub from above,
Kiss me with thy lips of love!
Bless the guileless soul that lies
Wakeful in thy brilliant eyes!
Scornful maidens love not true;
But ye little children do.
Ever till my life shall end,
I will be the children's friend.

December, 1859.

THEN AND NOW.

Once I was a blacksmith;
  I merrily did sing,
While I blew the bellows,
  And made the anvil ring.

While I held the iron
  Glowing in the tongs,
And thought of pretty damsels,
  To love I tuned my songs.

I thought of modest blushes
  Like the burning coal;
Then had real happiness
  Possession of my soul!

My mind was not distracted
  With the love of fame;
I cared not for high honors;
  I wished not for a name.

But now I am a student;
  O'er musty books I pore;
My watch-word now is " Glory;"
  My peace of mind is o'er.

Every star that twinkles
Seems to say to me,
" There is a brilliant future —
An immortality !

" Slumber not, O student ;
Let each rising sun
Find you farther onward
In the race you run.

" Each sun will shine more brightly,
As shorter grows the road,
That leads up to the lofty seat
Beside the Throne of God."

October, 1859.

TO DELIA.

Love's rough sea I 've waded through;
Now, capricious maid, adieu!
I, like Moses, now rejoice, —
Raise in grateful song my voice!
Glad I am I 've passed the sea, —
I rejoice that I am free!
Welcome desert wilderness,
Welcome hunger, thirst, distress,
I can bear to meet the worst!
Waters sweet shall quench my thirst,
Gushing from the flinty rock
At the rod's commanding stroke; —
Shall eat manna from above,
Sent by one requites my love.
Now I on a ram's horn blow, —
See, I conquer Jericho!
See, the walls fall to the ground
At the formidable sound!
While the battle rages high,
See the sun stop in the sky!
Soon possess I Palestine,
Lovely land of corn and wine.
When the conflicts all are past,
Happy shall I be at last!
Now I stormy Jordan stem;

Now rebuild Jerusalem ;
Now I fell a cedar grove, —
Build a temple to my love,
Fairer than the one of old,
Glistening with purer gold ;
Where I raise a holy shrine,
Worship there my spouse divine ;
To her sweeter songs I sing
Than sang Solomon the King.
So, perfidious maid, adieu !
I can scorn as well as you.

1859.

11

JENNIE.

Like Jesus, then, is Jennie meek ;
  Like Him, she 's ever kind ;
With truth and candor doth she speak ;
  No guile is in her mind.
No pride, therefore, no cold disdain,
  Yet conscious of her worth ;
There 's naught can make true greatness vain,-
  Her modest eyes meet earth.

When falls the gentle summer shower,
  It purifies the air :
Such is this pure-souled damsel's power, —
  No " thought infirm " stays where
Her presence is. A dew-drop pure,
  Her heavenly mind appears ;
I would no pain she might endure, —
  And live a thousand years !

May, 1860.

TO JENNIE.

JENNIE, may I be thy knight;
Go abroad for thee to fight;
Battle in the tournament,
Hither by my lady sent;
Battle bravely for renown,
Battle to obtain a crown —
Laurel wreath about my brow?
Say yes, Jennie, say it now!
I will stoutly fight for thee,
But shall surely claim my fee, —
Surely claim for my reward,
My sweet Jennie's kind regard.

June, 1860.

TO THE SAME.

Love, in the lines I now indite,
   I would to thee impart
A view, not of the outer world,
   But of my happy heart.

All's peace and joy! No cruel wars
   O'er its delightful fields;
The birds are singing; spring is there;
   The rose its fragrance yields.

One glorious little bird of light
   Hath builded there its nest;
'T is like the Bird of Paradise —
   So bright its plumèd crest.

Were it to spread its heavenly wings
   And fly away — how soon,
Ah, me! would be convulsed, destroyed
   The world whence it had flown.

Uriel, the archangel came
   On a sunbeam from above;
The messenger from high to earth
   Descended as a dove.

This little bird — this dove of mine —
  It is an angel bright;
From high a messenger to me
  Of blessing and delight.

May, 1861.

TO NANNIE.

WHAT care we for the world, Nannie, —
  The smiles or frowns of man?
A world within ourselves are we, —
  Thou art its glory, Nan.

Adam lived with Eve, Nannie,
  One woman lone and man
Upon the earth; and happily
  They lived, and we shall, Nan —

Shall live as happily, Nannie,
  Though far from walks of man;
For will not Nannie still love me,
  And I still love my Nan?

Nov. 7, 1861.

TO CLARA.

Had I loved you, I'd have told you —
   Told you, Clara, long ere now;
Would have sighed oft to behold you;
   Would have made an earnest vow.

I have never sent you token;
   But like Phæon fled away;
Ever to you I have spoken
   Kindly; I'm your friend to-day.

Nor can ever kindly feeling
   In my heart give place to wrath, —
And I now before you kneeling,
   Would strew flowers in your path.

Once I said "I am your brother;"
   Spake with feeling heart and true, —
There can nothing ever smother
   This my high regard for you.

But I cannot say "I love thee;"
   Cannot say "Thou art my dear:"
If there is a God above me,
   He my earnest words will hear.

Gentle sister, may no sorrow
  Ever sadden thy kind heart;
But may each returning morrow
  Come with joy, with joy depart.

June, 1860.

FRIENDSHIP.

WHAT a sacred tie is friendship!
Tie that never should be broken;
Never, never, never broken!
And it never *can* be broken,
If it truly has united —
Truly, truly, truly fastened
Kindred hearts but once together.

What a brilliant spark is friendship!
Read of Pythias and Damon; —
No disasters, no misfortunes;
Not the power of man or demon,
In their bosoms could extinguish
The bright spark that God had kindled.
Could they scorn at one another?
They would *die* for one another!

June 20*th*, 1857.

SERENA.

"Hark, they whisper; angels say
'Sister spirit, come away!'"

Thus the angel voices speaking,
  Bade Serena come away;
O'er the dark earth they were seeking
  Those to bask in endless day:

And they found the lovely maiden,
  Fairer than the flowers in bloom;
Bore her spirit to far Aidenn;
  Left her body in the tomb.

While our hearts o'erflow with sadness
  That we see her face no more, —
And while e'en a ray of gladness
  Seldom reaches this dark shore, —

She is with the Mediator,
  In the mansion of delight,
'Neath the smiles of her Creator,
  Far away from gloom of night.

Do we wish her back, to languish
  On a bed of grief and pain?
Oh, to hear her moan in anguish, —
  Do we ask her back again?

No, oh no; we wait the greeting
  In the happy realm above;
All the "pure in heart" a meeting
  God hath promised in His love.

August, 1857.

CASTE.

Away with caste! The humblest man, when free,
   Holds prouder rank in life than lord or king!
   In all that marks the man, (so poets sing,)
The poor surpass the rich. How fervently
The laborer loves the children on his knee!
   His honest heart — an overflowing spring!
   He 'd freely give his life an offering
To save his country's flag and liberty.
He read of Marion, when he was a boy;
   He heard how heroes fought at Bunker Hill;
His home, his wife, his children are his joy;
   Hope swells his heart. Perhaps his offspring
     will
Win wreaths of fame. He says, "I toil for
     bread;
My sons may strike for honor when I 'm dead."

BEAUTY.

GREAT Linnæus did oft, we know,
On long and tiresome journeys go,
To see the plants that far might grow;
And once, 't is said, he travelling found
Such pretty flowers, he kissed the ground:
Yes, he bowed down and kissed the earth,
Because it gave such beauty birth.
The lily blushing to the breeze —
Are kings arrayed like one of these?
The human form has grace divine;
There 's beauty in the towering pine;
The lovely lake with beauty smiles;
There 's beauty in the lonely isles;
The stars with beauty shine by night;
The sun is with his beauty bright;
'T is Beauty paints the evening skies;
There 's beauty in a damsel's eyes;
Behold the waves of ocean roll
Terrific to the human soul!
Yet there is beauty in those waves;
There 's beauty in earth's deepest caves;
And in the forkèd lightning's play,
And in the evening twilight gray;

And in the rugged mountains old;
And in the glistening iceberg cold.
Yes, Nature dresses all things fair;
Bright beauty 's blooming everywhere!

1860.

WESTWARD HO!

I 'LL go; why need I here remain?
   This land must not contain me long:
I 'll go; my thoughts are bent on gain;
   I 'll join the westward-moving throng.

I 'll go; for what is empty fame?
   I hate thy chains, O poverty!
I 'll go; 't is but at best a name, —
   Let me from want and duns be free!

I 'll go; I 've wakened from a dream;
   A bubble 's changed to empty air:
I 'll go; renown 's not worth, I deem,
   A drop of sweat, a moment's care.

I 'll go, and delve deep into earth;
   I 'll seek the "dust" — the shiny ore:
I 'll go; I crave not countless worth,
   I ask a competence — no more.

I 'll go; in some sequestered spot,
   'Neath California's pleasant skies,
I 'll build for me a modest cot,
   And claim Beatrice as my prize.

There will I live, and love, and sing,
  And rear the fig-tree and the vine,
While on me smiles perennial Spring,
  While for me flows the ruddy wine.

I 'll sing how mountain streams do flow;
  How skip the goats on rocks above;
How melt on high the hills of snow, —
  Sing to Beatrice of true love.

I 'll go; I hate the endless prate
  Of demagogues; their endless strife
For place and power in the State;
  I 'll go and lead a recluse life.

I 'll go; away from fashion, pride;
  Away from pasteboard pomp and show:
I 'll go gain happy home and bride, —
  There 's naught here worth a tear, — I 'll go!

April, 1860.

HOPE AND DESPAIR.

ARE my bright days now at an end?
Will Hope no longer me befriend?
Shall I no longer in her trust,
But bury up my mouth in dust?
I, often, since I was a child,
By her sweet voice have been beguiled.
She pointed gently with her hand, —
" Boy, Learning's temple there doth stand;
See, 't is conspicuous on yon hill;
Go climb and enter, if you will.
To you her gates will wide unfold;
Her treasures richer are than gold;
And if you conquer grim Despair
You will obtain a goodly share.
The dreadful giant guards the way;
Be clothed in steel; the monster slay!
Let modest Virtue be thy guide;
And look with scorn upon vain Pride.
Fame's temple also stands in view,
And you may enter therein, too;
For you are human; and all others,
The mightiest men, are but your brothers."

Thus Hope from me, an orphan boy,
Stole sweet contentment — heavenly joy!
I 've tried to climb the rugged way! —
Despair I battle with to-day.

1858.

HOW A YOUNG WRITER IS ENCOURAGED.

Indeed, young man, it is a crime
To waste your youth dabbling in rhyme!
Why do you not o'er Blackstone pore,
And fill your head with legal lore?
Because, hard is the poet's lot!
I'd rather be a drunken sot,
Than such a beggar on the earth;
For not a penny is he worth!
And he must lead a single life;
For how can he support a wife?
True poets sing alone for fame;
But who can live upon a name?
If you should gain the poet's meed —
(And are you likely to succeed?)
Like the chameleon, you must feed
Upon the "gentle zephyrs" — air!
And such, in truth, was Dryden's fare;
And such was Goldsmith's, Milton's, Burns',
Such ever is the bard's returns;
Whilst all the fame he gains, he earns;
For is he not deserving fame,
Who thus will live slave to a flame —
Absurd desire, that men may praise
His name through all the coming days?

One that was guilty of this crime,
Did he not die before his time?
Yes, the lamented Chatterton,
Britannia's most gifted son,
Took arsenic rather than ('t is said)
Die from necessity of bread!
Another of her sons of song —
Did he not fast, say, rather long?
He begged a loaf to save his breath;
Devouring it, he choked to death!
The greatest poets have been poor;
E'en Homer begged from door to door,
A life of sorrow Fate decreed
Tasso — imprisonment and need.
Better renounce a foolish lust,
And go to digging for the " dust,"
Crushing the quartz-rock, and be great;
Gold will gain honors in the State.

1860.

THE BIRD.*

WHEN I was a little boy,
I do remember, and it ever will
Remain deeply impressed upon my mind,
How with a playmate I, in wanton sport,
Stole from a nest some little, unfledged birds.
The mother bird
Had left them, as kind mothers sometimes leave
Their little children when they go from home, —
Left the little ones at home.
We came upon them
While we were rambling through the joyous
woods,
In search of balls that grow on little oaks, —
Spotted balls,
That crack when pressed between your hands,
Like mimic guns,
Or silken lash upon a coachman's whip.
My playmate said, " Hark, hark, I hear a chirp!"
We looked and saw, and then we climbed
And snatched them from the nest.
Their beaks they ope'd,
As if they thought we'd come to give them food.
They little knew

* The author's earliest essay in verse.

What boys would do, whose minds had never yet
Been taught to think how God has made
　　　The life of e'en a bird
As dear to it as ours to us; and how
His care supports the sparrows as they fall;
　　　And how
He smiles, when looking down upon the world,
　　　Sees all,
All happy, — birds and every living thing!
The world He made to be a world of joy;
All Nature smiles; the little flowers look gay;
And in the hearth the cricket happily chirps;
The brook flows, murmuring ever joyously,
While the silvery minnows listen its sweet mur-
　　　mur;
　　　With busy fins,
They happ'ly play beneath its dancing waves
Which sparkle in the sunlight.　And the sun
Sends forth its rays to beautify all Nature;
　　　It gives the beauteous hues
The poet's fancy loves to dwell upon.

　　　All Nature is but beauty;
And every living creature seems to say,
"I 'm happy when left as God has made me."
　　　And so
The little birds were happy in the nest,
　　　And soon,
In the transparent air, had soared aloft.
Beneath them would have stretched the smiling
　　　earth,

Concave to them in form, and dotted o'er
      With prairies,
And lakes, and lofty oaks, and mountain peaks,
Cities and temples, built in ancient times.
But we with ruthless hands bore them away, --
Away for sport! Joined by a noisy host
Of other boys as wicked as ourselves,
Our sport was of the gladiatoral kind.
How pitiful the little birds did cry,
When tossed by our rude hands high up in air!
They flutter, and fall hard upon the ground.
Now hands are clapped; a joyful laugh is
      raised ;
        A shout,
"Who first can get the bird and toss it up!"
Now, now we rush; the bird is snatched and
      torn ;
Another rush, — "'T is dying; throw it down!"
I staid, I know not why. I said, "I'll see
How much the little bird is hurt,"
        And took it up;
And oh, its little eyes it turned upon me,
        And the look it gave
I never can forget! It seemed to say,
"You wrong me, little boy." The tears ran down
My cheek, and fell upon its feathers; —
"Forgive me, little bird," said I, "forgive!"
Quivering in my hand, it died. How stricken
        Was my heart! I sought my home;
The little bird I carried with me;

My gentle sister made for it a shroud;
And in the garden, 'neath the apple-tree,
I dug its grave; and I, in wanton sport,
Again ne'er harmed a little bird.

May, 1856.

TO A FRIEND.

LIFE is before us a broad and wild prairie;
  While rambling o'er it at youth's early dawn,
Crossing obscure pathways where, often, unwary,
  Those now no more have joyfully gone —

Let us pause and then ask: "For what are we
      seeking?
  Only the flowers that come in our way?
Or, as bold pioneers, to *do work*, plainly speak-
      ing
    For those who come after: ' *We dwelt here one
      day?* ' "

To *work* is our purpose; to leave an impres-
    sion,
  That never the finger of Time can efface;
To give to our virtues a sun-like expression,
  That never, no never, a spot shall disgrace.

We would possess that noble ambition —
  The wish to excel in good deeds to man-
      kind;
And at all times, in humble submission,
  Willingly kneel at the altar of mind.

At the shrine never bowing of sensual pleasure,
  Supreme on the throne must the Intellect
    reign :
The Intellect ! Ah, this beyond measure
  Exalts us above the wild beasts of the plain.

May 16, 1857.

THE END.

www.ingramcontent.com/pod-product-compliance
Lightning Source LLC
Chambersburg PA
CBHW031110020726
47495CB00007B/2135